MW00963380

Deadly Choices

WhoooDoo Mysteries
A division of
Treble Heart Books
1284 Overlook Dr.
Sierra Vista, AZ 85635-5512
http://www.trebleheartbooks.com

Published and printed U.S.A.

ISBN: 1-932695-06-0

Thank you for choosing
A great new
WhoooDoo Mystery

Deadly Choices
by
Jeannie Spallone

WhoooDoo Mysteries
is a division of
Treble Heart Books

Dedication

I dedicate this book to my husband, children, and a furry white mutt named Marshmallow.

Acknowledgements

A heartfelt thanks to Paramedics Christine Mullally, Sarah and Mary, formerly of the Chicago Fire Department, for exemplifying the steel nerves and dedication necessary to rescue the vulnerable on the mean streets of Chicago. Thank you to Firefighter John Summers of the Broadview Fire Department; without your input the in the beginning, this book would have been a figment of my imagination. Thank you to the Cook County Police Department, Cook County Coroner and the Cook County State's Attorney's Office for making sure the details were completely accurate. Thank you Ernie Schweit for giving me my first foot up at the Daily Herald, the Creative Club for being the great sounding board, Rob Walker for mentoring me in this year of publication, Viki Rollins and Eric Cherry from Twilight Tales for calling me up to the mike and cheering me on, Barb Schneider for being the best editor ever, and Lee Emory for giving me the opportunity to, "Bring it on!" In every birth, it takes a village....

Chapter One

Warning lights unlit, siren silent, Ambulance Number 60 careened down fog-drenched streets in the pre-dawn autumn darkness on its return to the firehouse.

Some unseen radar directed the driver as she deftly maneuvered the ghost-like rig down West Madison Street through a maze of shattered liquor bottles and discarded syringes.

The ambulance soundlessly streamed past derelicts pasted on a backdrop of scarred buildings. Replenishing supplies in the back of the rig, paramedic trainee Beth Reilly stole a glance at the driver. She grimaced as her paramedic officer pulled a sandwich bag from her jacket. Angie often relied on that white stuff in her baggie to anesthetize herself against an avalanche of shootings, beatings, and vehicle collisions.

After five years as a nurse in Vietnam, followed by twelve years as a paramedic with the Chicago Fire Department, Angie Ropella seemed to delight in all forms of human trauma.

Knuckled in-between 24-hour stints of stabbings, multi-vehicle collisions, and assaults was an assembly line of little old ladies forgetting their insulin, yuppies jogging into cardiac arrest, and winos urinating in doorways.

Beth quickly averted her glance as Angie smirked at her through the rearview mirror. Her face still felt hot with shame after the tongue-lashing she'd received earlier that night.

She had efficiently resuscitated a drug addict lying half-dead on his bungalow porch as neighborhood kids hopped over his unconscious form in a midnight game of tag.

But the next fiasco had completely unnerved her. A scrawny seventeen-year-old kid in an oversize leather biker jacket had been weaving his motorcycle back and forth across four clear lanes of traffic when his luck was stolen by a black Toyota traveling southbound down Lake Shore Drive.

"Where's the body?" asked Beth, a former medical librarian.

"The kid must have been a human slingshot. Probably hit a tree and bounced into an oncoming lane of traffic. Let's check out the median strip," Angie said, grabbing a backboard. "Don't forget your gloves."

Extracting a pair of latex gloves from her pants pocket, Beth scurried to match Angie's long strides. Six weeks into her job, she had no intention of contracting AIDS.

About fifty feet north, a tree lay broken in half. The limp body of a kid in a motorcycle helmet sprawled across the adjoining median strip. Carefully, the paramedics fastened a cervical collar on him with Velcro™, then lifted the broken body onto the backboard. Upon applying a tourniquet to halt the bleeding from his leg and splinting several broken bones, they gently placed the boy on a stretcher and boosted the gurney into the ambulance.

"Oh, man," Angie said, groaning. "Check out this bone sticking through the kid's thigh. As if he won't have enough grief with a fractured pelvis, severe neck and back injuries, and a fractured skull."

After one look at the mangled body, Beth vomited all over the back seat. Angie just grinned.

"You gonna be a medic, Reilly, you can't keep having these little accidents. Clean it up. Then keep the kid company back here. I'll drive."

Up front, Angie picked up the radio. "This is Ambulance 60. We've got a trauma bypass and are en-route to Masonic."

The early morning weekday scramble had already kicked in as Angie switched on her illegal boom box to some old Led Zeppelin. Flipping on the siren and lights, she expertly weaved the red and white rig through a maze of congested traffic. She zigzagged around buses that suddenly jutted out in front of her onto Halsted and Clark. Cab drivers leaned on their horns while joggers sprinted off to work and the unencumbered meandered home from all-night bars.

Sirens screeching, Angie drove as quickly as possible but the fog and congestion held her back like a dog in quicksand. "Oh, fuck, son-of-a-bitch. Damn bus drivers don't give a shit about a life in danger."

Lights and sirens still whirring, Ambulance 60 finally pulled up the ramp to Illinois Masonic Hospital. Angie jumped out and ran around to the back of the ambulance, yanked open the doors, and wheeled the gurney into the ER where the trauma team waited.

***

Beth was wiping down the back of the ambulance with peroxide when Angie poked her shoulder.

"Listen, I got to take a pee and get some supplies. Why don't you jump-start the paperwork, then we'll split for tacos?"

"Sure. Meet you back on the ambulance. I mean the rig."

Pushing the empty gurney out through the double doors, Beth considered confiding in her best friend Sue Dotson about yet another of Angie's cocaine breaks. Nix that idea. The Evangelical foster care mom's familiar refrain was, "That woman sins against her body and should be reported."

After fourteen years as a medical librarian for the University of Chicago, Beth could spout drug statistics in her sleep, but she'd already memorized the fire academy's unwritten code: never pimp on your partner.

Whenever she felt guilty about not squealing, Beth reminded herself that Angie was a dedicated professional whose performance was always top notch. No one had ever reported the paramedic's coke habit. Besides, she had a lot to learn from the former Vietnam nurse whose heroic performance in saving lives could fill a textbook. So, she remained silent.

Once in the hospital laboratory, Angie allowed herself a whiff of congratulations from the white stuff in her Baggie. She grinned at her reflection in the mirror. "You were really on top of your game tonight!" Grabbing another backboard and more peroxide from the ER supply cabinet, she headed back to the rig.

Flicking on the boom box to some old Stevie Wonder, Angie steered the rig out of the parking lot and into the fog-laden night. The ambulance silently streamed down the empty streets, past abandoned warehouses and lots littered with broken liquor bottles. Beth looked up from straightening supplies to see Angie peering at her through the rearview mirror.

"Amazing the kid survived at all, what with the damage to his kidney and spleen!" Angie commented.

Beth nodded. Wait a minute. Was she getting paranoid or was her paramedic officer actually mouthing "wuss" into the mirror? Beth's face felt hot. She'd made it through textbook, strength, and skill training with top honors, but she still turned to mush at the sight of crushed bones and blood.

She was wracking her brain for a curt response when the ambulance slam-banged into a hard object, knocking her to the floor.

Up front, Angie was pinned against the steering wheel screaming, "Oh, shit!"

Chapter Two

What had they hit? Stomach churning, the paramedic trainee struggled into a sterile set of rubber gloves and leaped off the stalled ambulance.

A young woman, about eighteen or nineteen years old, lay sprawled out in a pool of blood that also oozed from her ears. Attempting to still her panic at the sight of so much blood, Beth focused on clamping the pressure cuff onto the patient's arm. Noting the dangerously low blood pressure, she flipped back the girl's eyelids; unconscious, seizing, bloated belly. Palpitating her patient's abdomen, a sudden gush of fluids spurted out. Lifting the girl's dress, Beth gasped as a tiny head emerged through the girl's vagina.

Tentatively rubbing her ribs, Angie jumped from the ambulance and squinted through the thick fog. "What the hell's going on? Did we hit a pothole? A dog?"

Beth ran back to the ambulance and grabbed her OB kit. "We hit a young mother whose baby is crowning!"

"Oh, my God," shrieked Angie. Running toward the patient, she was at the young woman's side, checking her vitals.

"What do we do now?" Beth asked nervously, peering over Angie's shoulder. Her head felt as though it was gripped in a vise and that nauseous feeling was threatening to overcome her.

"Check for ID."

Beth felt around the girl. No purse, no wallet. "Nothing."

"Probably a run-away." Angie paced, pounding her fist into her hand. "It's happening all over again."

"What are you talking about?" asked Beth.

"Countless lives lost because I couldn't put them back together. Vietnamese women and children being blown to smithereens as they try to outrun the bombs. But there was no escape. Now, because of my recklessness, this young mother is going to die, too."

Beth knelt to check the girl's blood pressure again. "The girl's fading. Should we radio the hospital?"

Shaking her head, Angie briskly stepped toward the rig. "I've had a clean record for fifteen years. No way am I getting called down on this accident."

Beth ran to catch up. "Angie, I need your help! She's unconscious."

"Well, that makes it all the easier. She's not going to move on you."

Frantically, Beth tugged at the paramedic officer's sleeve. "We can anonymously call 911 from the all-night diner!"

Slapping Beth's hand away, Angie climbed onto the rig. "And risk being recognized? You'll be all right. You know what to do."

"I can't work on the mother and deliver the baby at the same time!"

"Look, the girl's hemorrhaging through the ears. She's gonna croak any minute. You want my advice? Save the baby." A thin, steady rain framed each step as Angie hurried back to the ambulance, then climbed aboard.

Swiping at the raindrops clouding her eyes, Beth attempted to slow her breathing and focus on the job at hand. The self-relaxation technique of deep breathing had seen her through college exams, administrative bickering at the university, and recently her parents' fatal car crash.

An only child, Beth deeply mourned the death of her mother and father. She'd endured the endless array of condolence callers —students, professors, administrators, medical library staff before returning home to silence, the notes of her father's Mozart sonatas no longer floating upward from their old black upright piano.

Valedictorian of her high school graduating class at Loyola Academy, Beth sailed through her anatomy and biology classes at the University of Chicago. Her future as a doctor appeared eminent when both Northwestern and the U. of C. offered her a full medical school scholarship during her last year as an undergrad.

Her parents were thrilled with her academic success, yet Beth felt frozen by indecision. Medical school would be a pressure cooker. She might exit the experience brain dead.

Instead she became a medical librarian.

And now, here she was, a thirty-nine-year-old orphan. Two paramedic officers had, amidst speeding cars and trucks on the Dan Ryan highway, extracted both her parents from their crushed Toyota Celica. Her parents died before the ambulance reached the hospital. Amidst her grief, Beth recognized the heroism of the young man and woman. With no family or love life, she determined to close the book on her staid existence as a university medical librarian and become a hero-in-training.

Beth shivered in the early morning fog. Here she was, attempting to deliver a baby with no help from her superior officer. Beth placed a clean bath-size towel under her writhing patient, covered her with a sheet, waiting for the next contraction. Hopefully, the young mother would deliver her baby before the light rain-shower turned into a torrent.

The girl's pelvis arched as the baby's head turned clockwise. On the next contraction, Beth saw the baby's shoulders. She carefully caught the infant as it slid from the birth canal, and then cut the umbilical cord with a sterile scissors, clamping the leftover stump with a plastic clothespin. After suctioning the infant's mouth and nose, she lightly flicked the tiny feet. The baby shuddered through its first breath and Beth enfolded her in a clean towel.

Beth felt a thrill surge through her as she clutched the first baby she'd ever delivered. She had only to look at the mother and that joy disintegrated. The white bath towel underneath the young woman had turned crimson. Blood still oozed from the girl's ears, but her seizing stopped. The girl's pulse was faint. Beth hesitated. According to her triage training, she must save the more viable life.

The paramedic trainee glanced back at the ambulance. Angie was nowhere in sight but her fateful words echoed through Beth's brain: No use in delivering the placenta from a patient only a few breaths from death. Wrestling the bloody sheet and towel from underneath the woman, Beth zipped the infant inside her jacket and dashed toward the rig. Pressing the infant's tiny body against her breast as she ran, she felt the baby's mouth trying to root. An exhilarating sense of power swept over her: she alone had saved this baby from smothering inside her mother's womb.

As Beth cradled the tiny body, she wondered what to do. The girl was white, the baby cocoa. DCFS was quick to take a child but finding a home for a bi-racial infant was often a lengthy process. Some private agencies were experimenting with waiving adoption fees for African American families as an incentive to adopt. The program had mixed-results. And what about sexual and physical exploitation? Sue had shared many horror stories about the abuse her seven foster children had endured before being placed in her own loving home. Three of her children had been labeled as emotionally disturbed, and a fourth child, born with fetal alcohol syndrome, suffered from severe brain damage. Beth shuddered at the vision of the newborn infant she cradled being shuffled from one foster home to the next while the state decided what to do with her.

Attempting to breathe deeply through her stomach cramps, Beth visualized a moment, twenty years ago, during college when she'd broken-in to an animal shelter and rescued a nine-year-old Labrador Mix scheduled to be euthanized She believed God applauded her efforts because she'd never gotten caught. Only Sue knew the real story. Wait a minute! The answer to her current dilemma was Sue! Beth felt the emotional power of her past escapades surge through her body. She could bring the infant to her best friend. Sue could ask Reverend Luke, her pastor, to find a loving home for the baby through his church-sponsored adoption agency.

Shifting the infant to one side, Beth knelt down to check

the hemorrhaging young woman's vital signs one last time. Then, with a deep sigh, she arose and headed for the ambulance.

Climbing into the passenger side, Beth securely placed the swaddled infant between the seats. A glowing warmth settled in her stomach.

Angie was all sober nerves now. "Where's the girl?"

"You don't want to know."

"Oh, God. I killed her!"

"The blood has spilled, so stop whining."

Angie reached for the radio. "We got to radio in for help with the girl."

Suddenly Beth was overcome with a vicious rage unfamiliar to herself. She knocked Angie's hand from the radio. "Where was all that compassion when I was begging you to deliver the baby or assist the victim? You were only interested in avoiding a drug investigation."

"What about the baby?"

"I'll take care of her."

"You can't just take her like a stray pup!"

"I delivered her."

"Man, you're totally freaked out!"

Emboldened by her decision to keep the baby, Beth sensed her passivity dissolve in the fog outside. "Bitch! You're nothing but a crack head," she said in a sneering tone. "It's a wonder nobody ever turned you over to Internal Affairs."

The baby started to mewl inside the towel.

Hunching her shoulders as if to ward off further verbal attack, Angie switched on the ignition. "Let's get out of here."

Ambulance 60 slowly pulled off into the darkness.

* * *

"Where to now?" mumbled Angie, glancing at Beth.

"Back to E.R. at Masonic," directed Beth, her brain synapses firing new connections as she spoke. "We'll need some baby supplies."

"What are you going to say if someone stops you?"

"Don't worry. Nobody will stop me." Her mind flashed on the dog shelter raid she'd conducted so long ago, followed by her elusive spin into the night. Energy soared through her veins.

Angie steered the ambulance around to the back of the hospital.

"Leave the rig running so the baby stays warm," called Beth, as she jumped off the ambulance and sprinted through the sliding door facing the supply cabinet. A quick glance confirmed that the corridor was empty.

Out of habit, she muttered three Hail Marys as she rummaged through the supply cabinet for diapers and formula. Carelessly tossing other supplies aside, she finally found a handful of baby bottles filled with Pedialyte. Just as she stretched for the bottles, she felt a tap on her shoulder. Beth spun around to face Martina, the young Filipino who had recently been transferred to E.R. With all that heavy mascara, she looked like a Latin version of Madonna.

"Hey, what's happening?"

"Just looking for splints and ice packs. Guess you're out."

"I heard about that accident on Lake Shore Drive last night. The kid was a real Evel Knievel, huh?"

"He was broken up pretty bad," Beth hesitated. "Listen, I'm kind of in a hurry.

"No problem. I'll be back in a flash with your supplies," Martina said, scurrying down the hall to the cast room.

Releasing a deep sigh, Beth turned back toward the cabinet and hastily stuffed the Pedialyte bottles into her side pockets. Kneeling down, she picked up a small package of infant diapers. Then she grabbed a folded bed sheet from the stacked gurney outside the stockroom, wrapped the diapers and extra bottles in the sheet, and hurried out of the hospital.

The young hospital attendant emerged from the cast room, her arms laden with splints, ice packs and the extra bandages paramedics plastered on their patients as lavishly as preschoolers with stickers. "Hey!" she yelled as Beth dashed out the sliding door.

Martina dropped the load of supplies onto the bed sheet gurney. "That's one weird chick!"

It was 6:30 a.m. when Beth and Angie returned to the firehouse. Angie cut the ignition and leaned her forehead against the steering wheel. "I don't know if I can go through with this," she moaned.

Beth patted her on the shoulder. "It's no longer your problem, so just keep it to yourself. How about you go inside first?"

Angie nodded. Jumping off the ambulance, she circled around the vehicle. Nothing but the usual dents. Slipping her hands into her pockets, the veteran paramedic shuffled off toward the bright lights reflecting onto the parking lot.

Beth unlocked her vintage yellow Volkswagon Bug and gently placed the sleeping infant at the foot of the passenger seat. Freshly diapered and fed, the swaddled baby would be warm and safe until she finished the last 1 1/2 hours of her shift. She hoped Quinn would come in early to relieve her.

RJ Sloan was signing out as Beth walked through the door. "That motorcycle accident must have been a real pistol," he whistled, eyeing her blood soaked uniform. "You look like something out of Dracula."

"Halloween was last month," Beth groaned, shaking her head as she made her way upstairs to her locker.

Chapter Three

Upstairs, the late afternoon sun peaked, its shadow descending past the gossamer drape, as Beth sat cross-legged across her white down comforter. Gazing at the baby's long lashes and cap of black fuzz, she rocked her.

It had been twelve hours since Beth had arrived home with the baby, resolutely locking the door behind her and yanking the living room shades so hard their tassels shivered.

Guilt shattered her initial ecstasy. The baby's mother was probably lying in the morgue by now. Although there had been a sliver of a chance she might have saved the girl's life, she'd let Angie dissuade her. Yet God had enabled her to wrestle this innocent babe from her mother's dying womb. Dazed by the miracle of life, she soaked in the infant's sweet suckling sounds as it nestled to her breast. But a terrible anxiety hammered at her vow to provide a safe and loving harbor for this precious being rather than turn her over to DCFS.

Beth had repeatedly telephoned Sue throughout the day but her frantic voicemail messages had gone unanswered. Then she remembered that the foster care mom had taken her clan on an all-day outing to the Shedd Aquarium. Receiving a numeric page in the basement level was iffy.

The sun's rays reflected off the white walls framing the brass bed, momentarily comforting her. But the rapturous chords of a Mozart sonata emanating from her parents' antique victrola failed to alleviate her disquietude. Beth's tears dappled the baby's face. Once the police and media gobbled up the news of the dead girl and missing infant, her heroic efforts would lie buried. The whole city would galvanize to hunt her down. Thankfully her parents were no longer alive to witness their only child's transformation into a baby-snatcher.

The professors Reilly had insisted their daughter, the medical librarian, share their home, only walking distance from the U. of C. Beth enjoyed her parents' company, their stimulating dinner conversations about social justice and politics, but soon grew weary of her self-imposed isolation. Enter Jonathan Cornwell, a six-foot four-inch, ruddy-faced medical student whose sense of humor kept Beth in stitches. Although he was fun to hang out with, she missed the passion she'd felt for Michael.

Finally, after years of being pursued by the handsome doctor, whom her parents dearly loved, Beth decided to cast passion aside and retrieve her biological clock from storage.

Upon confronting her parents with her need to start a family, Beth watched in shock as her father wrenched Moonlight Sonata from the antique record player. Even more scary was the sight of her mother, her fingers spread across her face in a web of despair.

"You can't leave," her mother had wept.

"Jonathan received a job offer in Seattle. He's asked me to marry him. Don't I deserve a life of my own?"

"Of course you do," her mother whispered.

"Then what's the problem?" asked Beth, perplexed.

"When your father and I were attending grad school, we wanted to get married but my parents were afraid marriage would prohibit me from reaching my full potential. We planned to elope but were penniless."

"So we signed on with a university-sponsored genetics study, which paid graduate students for participating," her father interjected wearily.

"What does that have to do with me?" asked Beth.

"When I was pregnant with you, the doctors told us that the experimental medication we had ingested during that study would cause sterility in my children," her mother moaned.

Bile rose in Beth's throat. Choking it back she said, "But you had me anyway. Surely all the new advanced techniques can—"

"I assure you, your mother and I have explored all options."

A wave of sadness engulfed Beth as she realized the reason for her miscarriage so long ago. "We could always adopt."

"Honey, many of the children up for adoption have physical or mental handicaps. Is that what you want?" said her mother.

"You're flipping out," said Beth, grabbing her car keys. "I've got to get out of here."

"You're too upset to drive," her mother said. "Your father and I will go for a drive and meet you back here for dinner."

Grabbing his coat and hat, his hand on the doorknob, her

father turned to her and sighed, "Just know we love you."

Thirty minutes later, they had become statistics in a fiery multi-car collision on the Dan Ryan Expressway.

Chapter Four

It was still dark outside as the unmarked Chevy edged up to the paddy wagon double-parked on Madison and Green. The morning fog was lifting as Maggie O'Connor and Monroe Johnson, specialists from the city's Major Accidents division, exited their vehicle. Less than ten feet away, the bloody body of a young woman lie spread-eagled on the sidewalk.

Traffic specialist O'Connor popped a grape Jolly Rancher into her mouth as she approached the attending police officer. "What's up?"

Officer Zack Morrison was kneeling by the body. "Look's like somebody mistook this girl for a bag of garbage. Probably a hit and run. There's no sign of life. Her head is crushed."

Peering over the officer's shoulder, Maggie blanched. After eight years as a detective with the CPD, she still found it inconceivable that a vibrant human being could be reduced to a pile of mush. Being the only female in the traffic division, she was used to dealing with her angst privately. "You all right, Officer?"

"Yeah. Eleven years on the street, and this stuff still makes my stomach roll."

"This a dispatch?"

The officer shook his head. "Every morning at 6:30 a.m., we end our watch with breakfast at New Holiday Restaurant. My partner and I were driving past Madison and Green when we saw a prone body lying in a pool of blood."

"Hey, just hang in there, all right?"

Maggie hoped to work the scene before the early morning congestion complicated things. While Monroe snapped the woman and surrounding area with a full roll of colored 35 mm and Polaroids, she shined her flashlight up and down the street for any indication of skid marks or pieces of a grill or headlight.

Paula Larsen, an investigator from the medical examiner's office, soon arrivedto view and pronounce the body. Maggie stood by as Zack and his partner zip-bagged the victim and loaded her onto the wagon en route to the Cook County morgue."

Maggie watched as Dr. Kari Sarietta removed the body bag from the cooler and placed the remains, tagged "unidentified white female" on the examining table. Unzipping the body bag, the medical coroner gazed intently at the bruised face. "How swiftly the soul departs from the body."

"And we, mere mortals, its secrets to ponder," Maggie quoted.

"Ah, you, too, are a poet!"

"My minor in college. So, what do we have here?"

With needle-sized forceps, Sarietta carefully lifted a few stray white paint chips and shiny metal pieces from the hip area of the girl's dress and dropped them into a bite size manilla envelope. "Tire tracks on the clothing. The vehicle must have struck and run over her.

As she examined the corpse, Sarietta continued, "Blood in the abdominal cavity and a ruptured uterus."

Just then, four burn victims were wheeled in. "I apologize for the disruption. I will be in contact." Without further explanation, Sarietta thrust the unidentified woman back into the cooler until later.

Maggie climbed the stairs leading to the first floor and reemerged into the crisp fall morning. Monroe was waiting for her outside. "How did it go?"

"Nada. Sarietta's up to her hemline with bodies. Probably from that four-eleven fire we saw on the way here. Says she'll get back to us."

The day after the accident, Angie called in sick and spent the following seventy-two hours locked in her studio apartment, immersed in a cocaine stupor.

Emerging from her self-induced fog, Angie inched herself off the floor and propped her arms on a leather footrest. Swiping the web of sluggishness from her eyes, she gazed around the living room: overturned chairs, shredded food wrappers, and a dirty ice cream bowl. Her white angora cat pressed against her, purring piteously. "Poor baby," she said, hugging the ball of white fur. "Your bad mama forgot to feed you!"

Dragging herself into the cubicle her landlord called a kitchen, Angie reached for a can-opener and dumped three six-ounce cans of chicken livers into the cat's bowl. She grimaced at the smell. Pulling herself up to the refrigerator, she extracted a quart of milk.

"How could I have let Beth, a paramedic candidate of six weeks, bamboozle me? I was a nurse long before that dim-wit was accepted into her first honor society. Shit. Who gives that middle-aged rookie the right to call the shots on my career?"

Angie held the cat to her as she crawled the few feet back into the living room and buried her face in the orange carpeting. Sunlight snuck through the faded black drapes.

"No way is Beth getting the chance to report me to internal affairs. She's going down for kidnapping that baby, and I'm going to enjoy planning the perfect set-up". She cuddled the cat. "The only question is how to tell Captain Paine. He'll try to can my butt when he finds out I was flying when I banged the rig into the pregnant girl and left her for dead. But if he decides to get vicious, I've got my own bag of surprises for him."

Peering up at the delicately-woven spider webs hanging from the corners of the ceiling, Angie smiled with glee.

Chapter Five

The Lord's Assembly Church in Uptown Chicago dispensed salvation freely. Its job placement program boasted an eighty-percent success rate. Its Children and Family Services Program offered counseling to pregnant teens and placement for their babies. And its kindergarten through twelfth grade religious school mingled equal strains of inner city and suburban youth whose parents, tired of condom machines in high school restrooms, date rape support groups, and discussions about AIDS as a heterosexual as well as homosexual disease, applauded the church school's strict enforcement of God's laws.

Many graduates of the thirty-year-old school had gone on to Wheaton and Trinity, eventually leaving the states to spread the gospel in Somalia, Trinidad, Bosnia, and the former Soviet Union.

While The Lord's Assembly was held in high repute as a religious institution, none but the church elders knew their weekly donations were being used to fund evangelical fringe groups in the bombing of abortion clinics.

The church elders had expressed concern that informing congregants about the Assembly's radical strategies in combating baby killers could negatively impact the church's financial status. So Reverend Luke had discreetly paid a visit to an underground fundamentalist group known as "Mercenaries of God."

The next day, while The Lord's Assembly Church congregants peacefully protested the Cook County Board President's decision to reinstate abortion at Cook County Hospital, a small gang of radical *right to lifers* broke into the Women United Medical Clinic a few blocks from the projects, stripping files from metal cabinets, pouring gasoline on the contents, and setting them ablaze.

About the same time as the abortion clinic was shriveling into ashes in the name of God, an Evangelical Christian in Pompano Beach took it upon himself to blow away a doctor who operated three abortion clinics.

"Great quiche, Wally," said Angie, clutching her red leather writing journal as she headed out of the lunchroom.

"That was egg salad," an indignant voice hollered back from the kitchen.

"Whatever."

"Hey, Ange," called RJ from behind. "You hear about Monday's ambulance hit-and-run near wino heaven?"

Drawing a deep breath, Angie shook her head. "Guess my sidekick and I were too busy trying to rebuild Evil Knevil on LSD."

"Oh, yeah. Your clone-in-training was punching in while I was punching out. Looked like a vampire."

"Busy night."

"Anywho, rumor has it the vic was a poor homeless kid."

"You ever decide to chuck the department, you got a fine future as a detective." Angie laughed uneasily.

"No joke," he agreed. "I could dig taking pictures of nude broads screwing around on their rich and famous husbands."

"I'll bet."

"By the way, you guys have problems batting down Evil Knevil? We were on a three-eleven on Seminary. Twelve people overcome with smoke inhalation. Closed down all the ER rooms."

Angie hesitated. "We got him into Masonic."

Just then, the alarm went off. "Ciao, baby," said RJ, sprinting up the stairs.

Captain Paine's office stood adjacent to the basement stairs. Angie hesitated, fingering the journal. In it was a complete account of the hit-and-run. "Do I have the guts to do this?"

Until recently, an intoxicated firefighter who killed a pedestrian while operating an engine would temporarily get transferred to "paper duty." But community activists had forced changes in the rules, and the days of a slap on the wrist were now extinct.

"Only two years left until my pension kicks in," she said aloud.

"You talking to me?" a voice called out from the office.Captain Julian Paine's door was open, his back to her as he searched a file cabinet. She paused. His silver gray hair accentuated the impeccably starched blue and white uniform on his imposing frame.

"Cat got your tongue?" Captain Paine snickered, turning towards the paramedic.

"And a good morning to you, too, Sir," Angie said, with a click of her heels and a quick salute. Comic relief was one of the few techniques known to produce a sour smile.

"Listen, unlike you paramedics, I got a job to do. You got something to say, say it," he said, tightening his belt as he glared at her.

"It was nothing. Forget it." She spun around on her heels and started out the door.

"You broads all expect to be treated with kid gloves," he sneered, turning back to his files.

Her knuckles reddened as she clutched the doorknob. "I've never asked you for special treatment. Just a little of the respect you show your male officers."

"And why would I do that?" the captain retorted.

"To show you're human.

"Look, Ropella, I've stomached your crap for fifteen years. Now I got to put up with that new paramedic candidate. There's no law going to change my opinion that girls don't belong in the firehouse. My guys need to concentrate on fighting fires and saving lives, not on a pretty pair of legs."

Angie stalked back into the office, slamming the glass door behind her. "Saving lives, Captain? Like the time you were driving drunk and backed your engine into a mother and child crossing a side street?"

"An unfortunate accident. The rearview mirror was blocked."

"—And killed them?"

"The department never faulted me."

"Only because three of your cronies sat in internal affairs."

"Careful, Ropella. I could suspend you for insubordination."

"Something like that happened to me, I'd be bounced off the department in less time than it takes you to take a shit."

The ruddy-faced fire captain leaned toward her aggressively. "You got something to tell me, Ropella?"

Angie shook her head. "I'm not going to fry my own ass."

"Then by all means, let me fry it for you." He picked up the telephone. "This is Captain Paine. I'd like to request an unscheduled drug test for one of my paramedics."

"To hell with confession being good for the soul," screamed Angie as she bolted from the office.

Having nestled the baby in a bassinet, Beth gently shut her car door and headed into the firehouse to pick up her paycheck. She gasped at the sight of Angie bursting out of Captain Paine's office like an orangutan freed from captivity.

The captain sat huddled over the phone, his face the color of strawberry jam, barking into the mouthpiece. Although she couldn't make out what he was saying, she could guess what had happened. Angie must have gone in to clear her conscience about the accident and the kidnapping.

Paine was probably on the phone right now, requesting an internal affairs investigation. Beth leaned against the wall, her heart racing. She'd try one last time to reach Sue. If unsuccessful, drastic action would need to be taken to keep the baby safe.

Chapter Six

Sue Dotson was one of those moms every kid growing up in the chaotic '90s of day-care centers, home-alone parenting, and sexual abuse hungered for as intensely as a new babe at the breast.

But ten years ago, her young husband's terminal cancer had obliterated her potential to fulfill God's will. After the funeral, Sue had prostrated herself in her closet beneath the shelves of shoes and purses and praised the Lord. Resolutely wiping her face with a tissue, the young widow grabbed her Victorian-style telephone from the nightstand and punched in Reverend Luke's private number.

"Reverend Luke," she sniffled into the telephone, "I want to become a foster mother."

* * *

Sue Dotson sat in the bay window overlooking the garden, laughing as Ginny and Joey pelted each other with fallen leaves. The sun peeked through a tree half-dressed in amber, casting shadows across a carpet of reds, oranges, yellows and greens. A robin paused atop the gazebo before commencing its arduous pre-winter journey.

Pivoting back to the table, Sue coaxed another "oatmeal choo-choo" into Paulie's mouth. At ten-months old, he was the most placid of her seven foster children. She nuzzled his chubby brown cheeks and lightly tickled him under the chin. With eyes the size of billiards, he didn't miss a trick.

The gospel music of Amy Grant floated peacefully through the room as Sue threw on an apron and started scraping away at the oatmeal-stained dishes. Reverend Luke had allowed all four of her school-age kids to attend his religious school, forty-five minutes away, without being consigned to the two-year waiting list. She'd been up since 5:30 a.m., packing lunches and shooing the kids off to school.

Within a month of her husband's death, Sue had become the proud mother of eight children, the maximum both The Lord's Assembly and the State of Illinois allowed for licensed foster care.

Through the years, Sue meticulously kept track of the dozens of children who, in a rainbow of color, ethnicity, and mental and physical health and handicaps, had passed through her loving arms on the riverboat to adoption or high school graduation. Lisa, William, Jennifer, Nina, and Mark had even gone on to college.

But every now and then there were children even Sue, with her infinite love and patience, failed to melt and mend. Last spring, she had humbly admitted defeat regarding Robert and Richard, whose torture of small animals would have impressed

Jeffrey Dahmer. Reverend Luke had transferred the boys to an Evangelical group-home for wayward boys.

Sue fasted for three days in mourning for her lost boys. But God had spoken to her once again, and on the fourth day, Paulie was delivered into her arms. His nineteen-year-old mother had been arrested for hanging his three-year-old brother, and the Department of Children and Family Services had remanded the dead boy's baby brother unto The Lord's Assembly. Sue had broken down into tears when Reverend Luke had personally brought the new infant to her home for "emergency care."

Emergency foster care usually lasted only three weeks before a child was switched to a more permanent home; yet in the last five months, Paulie's case worker had only graced them once with her presence, their privacy left intact.

Gazing at Paulie as he attempted to hoist himself into a standing position, "Soon you'll be all grown up," she murmured wistfully. When she recently approached Reverend Luke about adopting the baby, the minister mentioned that the church didn't allow single parents to adopt.

Noticing how the young clergyman's eyes often slid over her breasts when he spoke to her after Sunday services, Sue was convinced otherwise. But even if she succeeded in seducing Reverend Luke into allowing her to adopt Paulie, a steel albatross still blocked her path with DCFS's new thrust in seeking African American homes for black babies.

The doorbell's musical notes interrupted her reverie. Wiping her hands on her red and white checked apron, Sue grabbed Paulie. "Be there in a sec," she called out, hurrying down the ceramic-tiled hall past the living-room. She saw her best friend peering through the rectangular glass panes that bordered her front door.

"How ya' all doin'," Sue said, swinging the door wide open. Then she peeked at the bundle in Beth's arms. "And who is this little one?"

"I must have called you a hundred times yesterday. Why didn't you return my calls?" Beth said, struggling to hold back the tears.

"I'm sorry I missed you, honey. My answering machine must have been on the blink. Let's get you a nice cup of chamomile tea. Then you can tell me about that sweet little thing in your arms," Sue said, heading for the kitchen with Beth behind her.

Beth plopped into a flowered kitchen chair and un-swaddled the infant. "Sue, something horrible has happened. Do you promise not to tell?"

"Let me guess," Sue said, laughing. "Another Angie escapade?"

Beth frowned. "I need your word that whatever I tell you remains strictly confidential."

Setting Beth's favorite herbal tea at her fingertips, Sue rocked Paulie in her arms. "I'm sorry, honey. Just tell me what's irking you."

Beth glanced down at the infant nestled in her arms. "I kidnapped this baby."

"What?"

"I mean it. It was foggy and Angie, stoned as usual, banged into this homeless girl lying in the street. When I examined her, she was giving birth."

"Oh, my God!"

"The girl was hemorrhaging to death. I begged Angie to help me but she wouldn't."

"But you've only been on the ambulance for six weeks. How could she expect you to deliver a baby and help the mother at the same time?"

"She didn't want to spoil her pristine record. Anyway, the girl was unconscious, hanging on with her last few breaths so I focused on delivering the baby."

"You actually stole this child?" Sue screamed, immediately muffling her mouth so the kids wouldn't frighten. "Why, you wouldn't even smoke grass in college because you were so afraid of getting caught."

"Fear was the farthest thing from my mind. It's so strange, Sue, but while I was delivering this baby, I felt as powerful as Creation itself."

"That's no excuse to steal another woman's baby. The devil must have blinded your eyes."

"It was God who entrusted me with this baby's life!"

"What happened to the mother?"

"We just left the girl in the street. Angie wanted to radio it in, but I told her that if she said anything, I'd report her coke habit to Internal Affairs."

"This can't be the Beth I know. God's wrath will—"

"Don't act holier than thou with me," Beth snarled. "I doubt you'd think twice if that sinister looking Reverend Luke knocked on your door holding a healthy newborn and said, 'Sister Sue, the Church no longer cares that you're a single parent so we'll allow you to adopt this perfect infant. All you have to do is promise not to ask where she came from.'"

Sue sank down into her chair, silent.

"Now I'm asking you the same thing," said Beth softly.

"What do you mean?"

"Look, Paulie's case worker could wrench him from your arms at any moment. But you need no longer worry about loving so precariously. We could raise this baby together, our own version of joint custody."

"Are you insane? This child isn't a stuffed animal to share."

Propping her chin in one hand, Beth gazed into the distance, deep in thought. "The logistics are really quite simple. She could live with you during the week; that way I'd be free to work my three 24-hour shifts, and catch up on my sleep. She could stay at my place on the weekends."

"You talk about this child as though she was a pup you rescued from being euthanized at the dog shelter."

Beth's eyes misted. "You once said that a healer and a rescuer were two sides of the same coin."

"You've got to turn her into the authorities," Sue insisted.

"The girl had no I.D. Maybe she was a runaway."

"If her picture was on TV, a relative might come forward."

"No way. The girl was white, the baby black. Her family was probably from a small town and couldn't deal with having an unwed pregnant daughter. Imagine how they'd react to taking in a biracial grandchild?"

"You sound like a prophet of Satan! You can't presume to know that poor girl's story."

"Don't you see, Sue? Together, we can provide this baby with the love and security she deserves. Ruthie could share the nursery with Paulie. You'll be doing God's will, saving this child from languishing in DCFS or being placed in a potentially abusive foster care home."

Sue stared into space, lost in thought. "What about the other children?" Sue said. "I don't care about myself, but I'd be putting seven other lives in jeopardy. If something happens to me, they'll all end up—"

"Trust in the Lord. Isn't that what you always say?" Beth whispered.

"If I did keep this baby, it would be quite a risk. We never know when the children's caseworkers will show up."

"Last week you were complaining that you haven't seen the older kids' caseworker since Valentine's Day."

"What would I tell the children?"

"That you've taken in a new foster baby."

"Pediatricians want to see a birth certificate."

"I'll get one."

"Won't you be under police scrutiny because of the hit and run?"

"It was foggy that night. No one was around to identify the number on our ambulance."

"But eventually…"

Beth abruptly stood up, knocking the yellow kitchen chair to the side. "This is not Let's Make A Deal. My parents are dead and gone. I have no one. If you can't find it in your heart to take in this infant, I'll raise her myself. "

"Wait. If God has chosen me, just as He chose Mary to bear his only son, who am I to deny Him?"

"Will you do it?"

Sue bent down and gently sat Paulie in his playpen, among his musical toys. Straightening up to her full five-feet, two-inches, she took the infant from Beth's arms. Tears stinging her eyes, she held the baby to her. "You shall be a comfort unto me in my old age as it was in the days of the Lord."

"I said *joint custody*, remember?"

"Of course. I meant Ruthie will comfort us both." An hour

later, after Beth had gone, Sue pried four-year-old Ginny's fingers from the kitchen telephone and punched in the familiar number, just to make sure that she was doing God's will.

Chapter Seven

Monroe and Maggie, "Double M'" as they were called by their co-workers at Major Accidents Investigative Section, covered the three blocks to New Holiday Restaurant by foot.

"There was no ID on the body," said Monroe, looking straight ahead as he spoke.

"Maybe she was panhandling and a wino got lucky," offered Maggie.

The accident team walked into the greasy spoon and approached the manager. "How you doin'?" Monroe asked. "Listen, there's been an accident out here. Did you see or hear anything? Screech of tires or a car speeding off, anything like that?"

The old man shook his head and continued to wipe down the counter. Maggie turned toward the patrons, all of whom looked as if they'd panhandled the money for the coffee they were drinking. "Anybody alive in here?" she asked. No answer. "That's what I thought."

"So what else is new?" said Monroe, holding the door open for her as they sauntered back into the street.

By the time the two traffic specialists arrived back at MAIS, it was 6:50 a.m., and Day Watch was there to relieve them. Although the seventy-year-old former Kraft building now owned by the city had two workable elevators, Maggie and Monroe preferred racing each other up the marble staircase to Major Accidents on the second floor.

"You gonna fill out the report?" asked Monroe, breathing hard.

"Sure. I'll call you if I need you," said Maggie, puffing in short spurts the way she'd been taught in her Tae Kwon Do classes.

In her criminal justice classes at the University of Illinois, Maggie had initially sniveled about the dozens of case reports they had been required to hand in to the instructor. But the practice had come in handy in her last five years with the Investigative Unit.

Monroe had dropped out of college after his first semester, his dyslexia too much of a barrier to deciphering the written word. But even though his brain processed words backwards, Monroe's keen memory and problem-solving abilities had helped Maggie solve many a mystery. It was Monroe who had come up with the idea to have CPD scuba divers comb Lake Michigan for a missing vehicle following a domestic violence case in which an enraged husband ran over his ex-wife as she bent down to tie her running shoes.

As Maggie painstakingly filled out triplicate copies of her report, she smiled. She and Monroe shared a real symbiotic relationship with Billy and Chuck from Day Watch.

The hillbillies, as she liked to call them, really knew their stuff when it came to accident investigation. And they always contributed a fresh perspective.

Entering Fatal Case Number 93-602 into the daily log, Maggie wondered if the unidentified woman's death might be a homicide rather than a hit-and-run.

After filing her report, she looked in on her commanding officer. "Got a minute?" she asked, seeing Sergeant Letterman's wheelchair pulled up to her desk. Monroe was already sitting across from her.

The three talked about the body. "Keep me posted," said Sergeant Letterman, the commanding officer.

"How's Double M' doin' today?" Billy had come up behind them and effusively placed his arms around their shoulders as they walked down the hallway.

"Like you want to know," teased Maggie. While she enjoyed his jovial banter, she respected his uncanny ability to chisel away at the most obscure facts in a case until he came up triumphant.

"Where's Chuck?" asked Monroe.

"In the john. What's going down?"

"We got a young woman whose head looks like it's been through a meat grinder," said Maggie.

"She alive?" asked Billy.

"Not when we saw her last," said Monroe.

"Two street cops found her on Madison and Green. She's smashed up pretty bad. Looks like a hit-and-run," Maggie added.

"Got an ID?"

"Nothing," said Monroe.

"Where's the body now?"

"Probably still in the cooler," said Maggie.

"Don't you two give it a thought," Billy said. "Chuck and I'll put in a request for Crime Lab to fingerprint and photo the lady. Maybe we'll get lucky and she'll have a tatoo or scar.

Then we'll check in with Missing Persons and get back on the street."

"That's what I like about you guys," grinned Maggie. "Always ready for a new horror flick."

Maggie grabbed her personal belongings and checked her watch. "Come on, Monroe. If we hurry, we can still pick up some Egg McMuffins."

"Let's do it," said Monroe.

"O'Connor? There's a call for you," Sergeant Letterman yelled out her office.

Maggie snatched up the receiver to the old black telephone," Traffic Specialist O'Connor here."

"Officer, this is Dr. Sarietta. I meant to call earlier about ME 93-602, but I've only now gotten back to doing the post."

"What can I do for you?" Grabbing a legal pad and pen, Maggie mouthed "Saretta" to Billy and Monroe.

"Upon examining unidentified white female ME 93-602, it's obvious that she recently gave birth. The placenta is still intact. It would appear that a knowledgeable person was in attendance at the time of birth. Was there any evidence of a birth having taken place prior to or during the time she got hit?"

"The officers never indicated that a birth had occurred," said Maggie, turning towards Monroe and Billy with raised eyebrows.

"Where's the baby?" asked Sarietta.

"We're on it. Thanks for the call." Maggie hung up the telephone, a question in her eyes.

Monroe sighed over her expression. "Fine," said Monroe. "But can we still eat first?"

"Sustenance is important to all living things," called Maggie, as she and Monroe bounded down the marble staircase.

Chapter Eight

RJ was scrubbing down the steps when Beth pulled into the garage. Slamming the door to the rig, she called out to the ambulance driver, "Take it easy, Quinn."

"How's it going?" RJ asked.

"First dispatch, a nine-year-old boy slips down an elevator shaft. Where was his mother, right? Second, a toddler playing hide-and-seek with grandpa in the kitchen; he knocks into a pot handle, splashing boiling oatmeal all over his little body. But the third run is the piece d'resistance: a woman is washing a drinking glass when it shatters. By the time we arrive, she's calmly sitting on the street curb, a towel wrapped tightly around her hand. Blood is seeping around the towel edges so her little girl starts swiping at it with another towel. We get the woman to emergency. Winds up, she's got AIDS. And she let her own child wipe up her blood!"

"Um, I was looking for a one-word answer, not a novel."

Beth grinned. "Say, the garage looks Lysol clean!"

"Like El Cap-i-tan says, 'one can never be too clean, especially around a fifty-year-old firehouse that reeks of gasoline.'"

"Don't look now but I think the Cap's coming. Quick, wipe up that oil by my rig!"

"Wha?" RJ turned to look.

"Kidding!" called Beth, making a beeline for the bathroom. The smell of sausage and eggs wafted through the open door from down below. Sunday brunch was always a treat when Wally was doing the cooking; before signing on with the fire department, the engineer had worked as a chef at Hotel Niko downtown.

Beth knew she'd partake in a symphony of thick white bread smothered with blackberry preserves, fresh orange juice still sporting its pulp, and pancakes as thick as a ham sandwich, yet light as the flick of a horse's tail.

After she cleaned up, Beth meandered downstairs toward the kitchen. On the way, she peeked outside at the firehouse garden, designed and planted by none other than Captain Paine himself. Don was out in the English garden, weeding the multicolor irises and hyacinths. Gigantic urns housed dozens of hardy plants the City had donated to the firehouse last spring.

Beth stuck her head out the door. "Think this garden will immortalize the Cap when he retires next year?"

Don leaned on the weeder, wiping the sweat from his forehead. "At least it provides a nice camouflage for the barrage of drive-by shootings around here."

"Breakfast's ready," Wally called out.

They both headed inside.

"Good morning, sir," Beth said, sliding into her seat. Nonchchalantly, Paine tossed a bloody sanitary pad onto the table between the sausage and scrambled eggs. "This yours, Beth?" he asked.

Beth's face reddened. Without a word, she grabbed the sanitary napkin and fled from the kitchen..

Spiking a forkful of blackberry pancakes, Paine spat after her, "Women don't belong in the firehouse with their monthly soil."

"We've checked Cook County Hospital, every medical clinic in the area, the churches, the dumpsters, and all the street people in sight. Nobody remembers seeing a homeless girl or a newborn. How 'bout we get some coffee?" asked Monroe, rubbing his tired eyes as Maggie slowly guided the unmarked Chevy toward the Olive Mission.

"No way," said Maggie. "This thing's really got me going. I mean, a pregnant girl's got to stand out around here like a Mercedes. I get this feeling that whoever killed her took her baby."

"So let me get this straight. A drunk driver bangs into a pregnant homeless girl, stops his vehicle to assist at the birth of her baby then kidnaps the baby. That's a real logical scenario."

"I know it sounds weird, but I'm just going by instinct here. Anyway, someone's got to have seen the girl."

Monroe didn't answer.

"Okay, okay, we'll take a break after we interview the people at the mission," Maggie said.

Pulling up in front of the mission, the investigators noticed two men shivering against the cold night wind as they puffed on cigarettes.

"Hey, how's it goin'?" asked Monroe, flashing his badge.

"Just fine, man," answered one guy. "You got somethin' to drink?"

"Naw. Listen, there was an accident on Madison and Green

early yesterday morning. A pregnant woman was killed. You dudes see anything unusual going down last night?"

"Hey, man, weird things always happenin' around here. This one guy walk around with a bag over his head lookin' like a mummy."

"Right. Well, if you remember seeing a pregnant woman at the shelter or on the streets, give me a call," said Monroe, pressing a business card into his hand.

"Hopefully I'll have better luck inside the mission," said Maggie.

"Go for it," said Monroe, heading back to the car.

Less than a half-hour later, Maggie returned.

"You look like you just knocked over a drug pin for five mill," laughed Monroe.

Maggie tossed the car keys to Monroe and climbed in the passenger side. "Even better. The shelter coordinator remembers seeing a young white pregnant woman in here three nights ago. She was asking around for free clinics and adoption agencies."

"Terrific. Her name listed in the register?"

"She only registered under a first name— Violet."

"Bet you a fin that's not her real name," said Monroe.

"An old lady at the shelter said Violet took a liking to her, told her where she was from. But the old lady only remembers that it's some farming town in Southern Illinois that starts with the letter C. Violet told her the town was so small that one family runs the restaurant, post office, and funeral home."

"We can check out the sergeant's atlas for names of towns that start with a C, then fax the local sheriff a picture of the deceased."

"There are probably hundreds of small towns in Southern Illinois that start with the letter C."

"You start faxing from the beginning of the list, I'll start from the end."

"Someday we'll have Internet access and group e-mail."

"And someday Chicago's West Side will be rehabbed for the wealthy. Meantime, let's just do what we gotta do."

Monroe looked at her.

Maggie laughed. "After your well deserved coffee. I'll even pop for baklava."

Chapter Nine

Three weeks had crept by since the accident. Angie perched on the barstool, gulping her third dark brew as she waited for her connection. "Hey Joe, I ever mention I was a Vietnam battlefield nurse stationed in Da Nang?"

Wiping down the table, the bartender shook his head.

"My fiancé was an army doc. The Viet Cong blew his head off during an ambush."

"Tough luck!"

"I was a hysterical, a real mess. So a buddy of his gives me some white powder, tells me it'll help me forget."

"Did it work?"

"It made me what I am today: an addict. But I gotta say, Coke has really suited my professional life. It keeps the adrenalin going long after I've eked a body out from underneath a car or brought a diabetic heroin addict back to life with glucose and Narcan."

"Ever get nailed?"

Angie shook her head. "I had this partner recently transferred to a different firehouse. He used to say, 'As long as you do your job, it's none of my business.' In fact, my record's been unclouded until now."

"What do you mean?"

Hearing some hearty chatter, Angie glanced up to see two undercover narcotics cops enter the bar. "Nothing at all," she said, laying a deuce on the counter and heading towards the back of the bar. She waited as one of the cops ordered a Miller Lite, then casually followed him toward the back room flanking the pool table. Angie plopped her mug down on an adjoining table as Lou Martelli chalked the cues.

"How you doing, Angie?" the undercover cop asked, eying the billiards before him.

"Listen, I need another gram."

"You're kidding, right?"

"I know I owe you some money, but I promise I'll pay you back."

"Danny's calculations say you're three thousand in arrears."

"Some deep shit is going down, and I really need it, Lou."

"I've only let it go this far because you're such a great fuck."

"I'll do anything you want."

"It's too late, babe. Danny wants to haul your ass into the slammer, say we were working you undercover."

"Don't let him do it, Lou. I've only got two years until my pension kicks in; I'd lose everything."

"Pay your bill by Friday, and everything will be fine."

"How am I supposed to come up with that kind of money?"

"You're resourceful."

"Lou, I just got to have one more gram," Angie whimpered.

"Hey, why not? If you're going to hang yourself, another C-note won't make any difference."

His hand closed over Angie's palm. She stuffed the tiny Baggie into her jacket pocket, slurped down the last few drops of beer, and headed toward the door.

Swaying down the alley, Angie noticed a bank. She began to giggle. "How about I ask you for a loan to pay back my drug habit?"

She hadn't seen her alcoholic mother for years, and her father was long buried. Her only friends were the people she worked with, but she'd managed to divorce her habit from the firehouse.

Her head was pounding. Sitting down on the curb, she rummaged through her pocket for the tiny bottle of children's chewable aspirin. "Yuck, I hate pills but these taste just like candy."

She was so alone, like that runaway girl she'd left sprawled on the street. Angie slipped the pack of cherry flavored aspirin into her mouth and chewed until her mouth tasted of the sweet, juicy summer days when she and her friends would shoot marbles until dusk.

Glancing up and down the alley, Angie opened the tiny Baggie, thrusting its entire contents down her throat. Her esophagus burned furiously in protest of the dry white powder and she started to gag, but her airways soon became numb. Slumping to the ground, she saw a dove flitting off into the sunset.

* * *

Mercedes and Jaguars flanked Sue Dotson's circular driveway as Beth pulled up in her yellow Bug. Although she had taken a horticulture class as an undergrad, gardening wasn't really her thing. But Sue had prevailed upon her to come to the Sauganash Gardening Society's annual "Summer in January" social.

To appease Sue, Beth had driven grudgingly from Hyde Park to Sauganash. She also looked forward to seeing Ruthie. And she could talk about her philodendrons and diffenbachias, the only two species of plants she could manage to keep alive.

Locking the car door behind her, Beth glanced at her watch. Only 6:00 pm. Maybe she could rock Ruthie to sleep tonight in the nursery, a luxury she'd been too morose to consider in the post-accident days. She kept expecting to see herself on the 10:00 news, a kidnapper and murderer finally brought to justice.

Creating a new lifestyle with Baby Ruthie at the center of her universe had been miraculously simple, even though she had to scrap her original plan regarding shared custody. Beth might be a natural-born rescuer, but Sue was a natural-born mother. When alone with Beth, Ruthie cried herself into a frenzy. Yet she gurgled happily in Sue's loving arms. The two friends decided that it would be best for all concerned if Sue assumed full custody of the baby and she grew into the role of "Aunt Beth". With Sue at the helm, the baby's identity, or non-identity, would also be safeguarded.

A pediatrician friend of Reverend Luke agreed to provide medical service for the newborn until the misplaced original birth certificate was reissued. Little did he know that there was no birth certificate.

Beth's eyes shifted up towards the three-story mansion. So much for old money. Walking up the driveway, she noticed all the kids' bikes and toys had been hidden from sight, and the colorful chalk rainbows hosed off the sidewalk.

The screen door swung open. "I'm so glad you decided to come," Sue's voice rang out into the dusk.

"How could I refuse after the way you hassled me on the phone?" Beth complained good-naturedly, as she climbed the front stairs.

"A little friendly persuasion never hurt anybody. Anyway, you're going to have a wonderful time tonight," Sue said, black high heels clicking against the hardwood floor as she welcomed her friend into the house. "There's someone I'd like you to meet."

"I thought maybe I could see the baby first. It's been a whole week."

"The kids are playing with Ruthie upstairs. How 'bout you settle in first?"

Beth groaned. What was her friend up to now?

Sue slid the glass patio door open. "Beth, I'd like you to meet Eric Saunders," she said, her eyes twinkling. "He's an art history professor at your alma mater and a gardening expert besides. I already told Eric you used to be a medical librarian at the university but now you're a paramedic."

Beth's heart did an involuntary leap as her eyes latched onto the twinkling brown orbs of a thin, bearded man in turquoise shirt and jeans. Except for the color of his eyes, he could be Michael's twin. The guy was gorgeous, with long lashes and a warm, open smile.

The doorbell's melodic chimes echoed through the house. "Why don't you two just go ahead and get acquainted?" cried Sue, heading back into the house.

Beth nodded, trying to stifle the electrifying attraction she felt toward this stranger.

"Can I get you some punch? It's got a most unusual zing to it," said Eric.

"I'd prefer a glass of white wine, if there is any."

Eric opened a bottle of Pinot Grigio and reached across the buffet table for a clean glass. "So how does somebody transform herself from a mild-mannered librarian into a professional rescuer who dines on disaster?"

"Well, my parents recently died in a car crash. I was grateful for how hard the paramedics worked in an attempt to save their lives, so I decided to chuck my Clark Kent existence and train to be Wonder Woman."

"Don't you mean 'Bat Man'?"

"Ah, you are listening," she teased.

He looked at her incredulously. "It's not every day you get to meet a paramedic. It must be a trip never knowing if the next call is going to be an emergency or a hoax. Have you ever had anyone die on you?"

She paled. "Are you a plant for Geraldo Rivera?"

The bearded man sputtered. "I'm sorry I upset you. Please forgive my lack of manners."

Just then, Sue returned, flanked by a tall man in dark glasses.

"I apologize for interrupting, but I just wanted to introduce you to my neighbor. His lovely courtyard garden is one reason we voted him vice-president of the Sauganash Gardening Society. Julian, this is Beth and Eric. Beth is a paramedic."

Removing his glasses, the man smiled tauntingly. "I believe we've met."

The sound of the shattered wine glass as it tinkled onto the deck freed Beth from the shock of seeing him. What had she done to deserve this little surprise?

"I've got to go." Yanking a roll of paper towels from the kitchen sink, Beth dropped it into Sue's arms and bolted for the door.

"But you only just got here," complained Sue. "What's wrong? You're acting like a pit bull who's just taken a bite out of the mayor's behind."

Beth stopped. "I'm covering for Quinn at 10:00." She took a deep breath. "Listen, I don't want to spoil your party, but your friendly neighbor is the jerk at work who's making my life so miserable."

"Oh my gosh, you mean he's your captain? I'm so sorry. He told me he was a firefighter but with all the fire stations in the city, I never imagined."

"He intercepts my personal telephone calls, and once I found white bar soap smeared over my spare uniform hanging in the locker."

"That's terrible, but how do you know Julian did it?"

"It's not just me. He keeps his firefighters out on the street in between calls, raising ladders and practicing fire hydrant maneuvers for hours at a time."

"Why don't you complain to his supervisor?"

"That would be suicide. There's only two other female paramedics in our district, and if word gets out that I'm a squealer, the guys will make life miserable for us. I'm not about to lose my job after only three months with the department."

"Couldn't you go back to that private ambulance company?"

"I became a paramedic to save lives, not chauffeur nursing home patients back and forth to the hospital for glaucoma tests."

"Then I guess you'll have to pull in your quills and play possum," said Sue sadly. "Sweetie, do you still want to come up and see Ruthie?

"Of course." Beth's face brightened as she followed Sue to the now darkened nursery Ruthie shared with Paulie. "I thought you said she was up."

"I'm sorry, honey. Gina put Ruthie to sleep about fifteen minutes ago. You were in such deep conversation with Eric, I didn't want to disturb you."

"She's so beautiful," whispered Beth, peering through the door, marveling at the moonlight's glow glistening on the infant's ebony cheeks. "I just hope everything turns out all right."

"And why shouldn't it?" asked a voice from behind. Julian Paine's shadow flooded the room. Sue gasped and Beth's stomach did a triple-take, just like the time she arrived on a call to find a decapitated man sprawled in a tub of blood.

"Sorry, I didn't mean to frighten you girls. Perhaps I was too bold in following you up the stairs, but I just wanted to see more of your lovely home."

"I'm flattered," said Sue, quickly recovering her composure and grabbing his arm. "Let me take you on a grand tour of the upstairs. We'll have to tiptoe, though—the little ones are sleeping."

Blowing a kiss to Beth, she called out, "Talk to you tomorrow."

Running her hand lightly over the baby's fingers, Beth sighed, wondering how her friend could blithely go on with life as if nothing had happened, expunging the word "kidnapping" from her vocabulary as though it had never existed.

Beth hurried down the rose-colored staircase, and saw Eric waiting below. Remembering her earlier hasty retreat, she blushed.

"You dashed off so fast you forgot your scarf," he smiled, miming the moves of a French chef presenting a Cherries Jubilee. "The blue and purple swirls of the silk remind one of a Van Gogh."

Beth snatched the scarf. Then realizing what she'd done, said, "I'm sorry to run, but I'm filling in for another paramedic tonight."

"When can I see you again?"

"Sue's got my number." Beth grabbed her white wool coat from the hall closet and rushed out the door, letting it slam behind her. The last thing she needed was to get close to this good-looking stranger.

Chapter Ten

Fire Captain Julian Paine leaned back in the reclining chair in his private office, puffing on a fat cigar. His eyes thoroughly devoured each page of the Chicago Tribune's first edition, especially the accounts of Lloyd Perkins' arrest for child molestation.

North Shore teacher Lloyd Perkins was taken into custodySaturday accused of sexually molesting 11 students in his physical education classes spanning the last three years. Students told reporters that Perkins had threatened their lives if they told anyone what happened.

Paine's pleasant reverie was broken by a knock on his door.

"Yeah, what is it?" heasked, taking another puff on his cigar.

"Cap, we just got word from headquarters that Angie's dead," Wally said.

"She OD?"

"Why do you ask?"

"Come on. Just because I'm the commanding officer around here doesn't mean I don't know what's going down. Where'd they find her?"

"In the alley, a hundred feet from the Tumble Inn. The police think it could be homicide."

"Okay, thanks. I'll take it from here," said the captain, crushing his cigar in a red and black fire engine ashtray and ushering the firefighter out of his office.

Paine held his nose at the stale smell emanating from the gray metal locker. It wasn't the first time he'd had occasion to look in Angie's locker; he'd meandered through each firefighter's and paramedic's lockers over the years, just for curiosity's sake. This time he was lucky. Since she hadn't been on shift when she offed herself, her personal clothing was gone.

Spraying down the locker with Lysol, he accidentally scattered a handful of unframed three by five-inch photographs. Wiping the dust from the yellowed photos, he found one picture of a young Angie dressed in a nurse's uniform, arm in arm with a soldier. A second picture showed a group of young Vietnamese children all smiling into the camera. A third photo showed Angie dressed in Eastern Indian apparel and a headband, smiling into the eyes of another woman as they held hands outside a farmhouse. A more recent snapshot showed Angie in a black evening dress grasping the arm of a muscular guy in a black suit.

Paine recognized the man in the picture as Lou Mortella, a undercover drugs cop known to be dealing cocaine. "Did you knock Angie off because she owed you some big bucks, Lou?"

Paine took a last swat at the top shelf; a red leather diary fell to the floor. Unlocked. Previously unnoticed. Paine looked around. The locker room was still empty, the next shift not due to arrive for another half-hour. He peeked into the diary and a small piece of paper fell out. He bent to pick it up. The ink was blurred as he read:

I can't go on living with myself after knowing what I've done. When Beth snatched the baby, I should have reported it, but no, I was too fucked up about not making it to pension time. God forgive me for leaving the girl to bleed to death. I don't deserve to live, but I don't have the guts to kill myself.

The note was dated November 22, 1993.

Nice Thanksgiving gift, chortled the captain, stuffing the note into his shirt pocket and priming another cigar.

"You all right, Cap?" Don called from across the locker room.

"Oh, yeah. Real fine."

Back in his office, Paine began dialing the former police chief's telephone number on the old black rotary telephone. He searched in his top desk drawer for some Maalox or Tums. Stretching the short telephone cord out into the hallway leading to the firehouse kitchen, he leaned around the glass window.

"Wally, you out there?"

Wally was dipping individual slices of bread into a French toast batter and dropping them in the sizzling frying pan. "Need something, Cap?"

"A cup of strong black coffee."

"Sure thing," said Wally, rolling his eyes from behind the partition that separated them.

As Paine popped some Maalox, Paddy's wife Sarah picked up the telephone.

"Hallo? Who is this?" the hearing-challenged Sarah shouted into the telephone.

"Sarah, it's Julian," Julian shouted. "Is Paddy home?"

"No, he had to go downtown."

"Listen, Sarah, can you have him call me at the firehouse when he gets back?"

"I'll have him call you when he gets home." Click.

Hanging up the receiver, Paine clutched his chest, wincing. "Wally, my coff—"

"Coming, Cap," called Wally. Balancing the steaming cup and saucer across the newly washed floor. "Here we go, Cap," he said, stepping into Paine's glass office. "Jesus," Wally yelled, quickly setting the cup and saucer on the desk.

Wally bounded up the stairs of the firehouse to the apparatus floor where Quinn and Beth were playing ping-pong, the morning sun peeking over the firehouse. "The captain's on the floor! I think it's his heart."

With Quinn right behind, Beth ran down the stairs and swung open the captain's door. The captain lay sprawled on the floor, unconscious.

Moving the big brown desk chair aside, the she kneeled next to Paine and carefully rolled him on his back. Quinn took one look and ran back upstairs to get the blood pressure cuffs, the portable oxygen tank and mask, and the heart monitor. Struggling with his arms full, he ran back to the office.

Meanwhile, Beth shook the captain. "Cap, cap, wake up. Are you sick? Are you hurt? What's wrong?"

Quinn stumbled in with the equipment and unceremoniously dumped it on the floor. He placed the oxygen mask over the captain's face, turning the tank on to 15 liters, the average dose for an unconscious patient.

Beth placed the blood pressure cuff around the captain's biceps, pumping the bulb in her hand to inflate the cuff to 200, then slowly letting the air leak out. Releasing the bulb, she held the stethoscope to the captain's chest. When a crashing sound pounded her ears, Beth tightened the little knob on the bulb, pumping the cuff up to 260, then letting the air out slowly.

"His pressure's 220/120. Let's get him on the monitor. Where's the electrodes?"

Quinn unzipped the pouch attached to the monitor and gave Beth three electrodes. Unbuttoning the captain's shirt, Beth placed an electrode on each shoulder underneath the collarbone and the third electrode underneath his left ribcage. Grabbing the three multi-color leads, she attached the wires to the electrodes and hooked the captain up to the monitor. Pressing the "on" switch, she watched the monitor to see what heart rhythm would appear.

Quinn tied a rubber tourniquet around the captain's right arm as he searched for a vein to start an IV. While waiting for the vein to pop up, he tore off three pieces of adhesive tape and stuck them to the desk for quick access.

Beth gazed at the monitor. "His pulse is all over the place and he's throwing PVCs."

Quinn started the IV line, then taped the IV on the captain's arm. Beth grabbed a syringe of Lidocaine and stuck the needle into the IV's hub. "How much do you think the Cap weighs?"

"He's about one-eighty, one-eighty-five. Why don't we give him the whole thing?" said Quinn.

Slowly pushing the glass tube's contents into the IV line, Beth administered the Lidocaine. "How's his rhythm now?"

"PVCs are gone, and his heart rhythm's back to normal."

A small group of firefighters huddled in the doorway like football players at halftime."

Beth threw the ambulance keys to Wally. "Grab a couple of guys and get the stretcher down here. We've got to get the Cap to the hospital."

RJ and Don rolled the stretcher down the stairs and into the private office and lifted the captain into the stretcher and up the short flight of stairs.

After lifting the captain onto the rig, Quinn gunned the ambulance towards Northwestern Hospital, lights flashing and siren wailing and Beth activated the alarm to NorthWestern's ER. Perched on the jump seat, her knees bumping against the stretcher as the ambulance rolled over Chicago's potholes, Beth informed the intake doctor of the situation.

While reconnecting the tubing from the portable oxygen tank to the larger ambulance oxygen tank, she mumbled, "I should just let you die, you ignorant son-of-a-bitch." Overcome with remorse, she promptly mouthed Three Hail Marys.

Chapter Eleven

Lucy Clayman had just unlocked the door and carefully aligned her wet boots on the welcome mat when she heard the familiar buzz of the fax machine in motion. Shrugging out of her orange rain poncho and hanging it neatly on the maple coat rack, she stood gazing at the tiny red light as she smoothed her braid of long gray hair.

Faxes were few and far between in the Rackton Country Sheriff's office and usually dealt with a farmer's flooded cornfield or a cow-tipping. But even though Chilicothe, Illinois boasted only three-thousand innocent souls, Sheriff Lloyd Tanner believed in being up to date in technology, just in case the FBI ever needed his assistance.

Lucy yanked the completed message from the machine. The Williams Family, who had owned the town's only funeral home and restaurant for three generations, had donated a fax machine to the sheriff's office to go along with the new IBM computer they'd donated the previous year.

Fortunately, this latest trinket pretty much ran itself. She only had to keep track of the Sheriff's number when she needed to send outgoing messages and store an adequate supply of paper. Lucy's petite frame hardly made an indentation in the sheriff's plush black leather chair as she swiveled in front of his oversized walnut desk. The sheriff wasn't due back from his fishing trip until Monday, and Sam wouldn't be in until 10:00 a.m. Digging out a pair of Woolworth's reading glasses from her purse, Lucy brought the note close to her face. Scanning the return address of the Chicago Police Department, she muttered, "Whoee! Looks like the sheriff's finally lucked out." Peering into the smeared black type, she made a mental note to replace the ink as she read:

On November 23rd at 6:30 a.m., an unidentified, young whitefemale was fatally injured in what appears to be a hit-and-run. We have reason to believe that the victim, a/k/a Violet, may have resided in Chilicothe, Il.

*If you are aware of any young girl, possibly pregnant, who may have left your town recently, please contact our office immediately. *Photo of deceased victim follows.*

*Maggie O'Connor, Star *73509."*

Flipping to page two, Lucy flinched as her eyes focused on the battered skull. The girl's face looked frightfully familiar. Taking care not to damage the carbon photo, Lucy traced the small pert nose, wide cheekbones, and sensuous lips of her nephew's high school sweetheart. "Oh Violet, before you upped and disappeared, Matt was fixin' on askin' you to be his wife. His heart would be broken, seeing you like this."

* * *

The bells on the front door jingled as Sam Aarons pushed through the door as briskly as a west wind whipping over the cornfields. "How you doing this fine morning, Lucy May?" he whistled, wiping his shoes on the mat and shaking out his raincoat. "It's wetter than a baby's tears this morning, ain't it?"

Pulling up the shades in the office, Sam saw Lucy slumped over the sheriff's desk, quietly mewing like an injured kitten. "Whatever's the matter, hon?" he said, dragging a heavy wooden chair next to Lucy and protectively putting his arm around her shoulders.

Without a word, Lucy passed the fax to Sam. When he flipped to the second page, his jaw dropped. "Oh, my Lord."

Deputy Sam Aarons waited until after dinner to approach the Williams family with the unsettling news. He called his wife, Addie, to check on her and the baby, and told her he'd be a bit late for dinner, so not to wait.

Switching the radio dial full-blast to his favorite country music station, Sam began the three-mile drive out to the home of John Paul Williams, Sr. The deputy winced as "Achy, Breaky Heart" blasted through the darkness. Normally right up there on his list of "Top Ten," the song's lyrics reminded him of the emotional pain his visit would inflict on Violet's family. Yet Sam felt a slithering wave of self-righteousness that for the first time in three generations an Aarons, not a Williams, was finally doing the inflicting.

Ever since his parents had immigrated to Chilicothe after World War II, their Jewish background seemed of utmost importance. In third grade, two of his father's classmates put a note in his lunch bag, accusing him of being a "Christ killer." In sixth grade, three boys grabbed David after school as he was walking home through the cornfields. After taking turns pummeling David's face and stomach, Paul Williams, the leader of the group, had towered over his bloodied victim and spat out the venomous words David would never forget. "Too bad Hitler didn't finish the job, you dirty kike."

When Grandpa Benjamin appeared at the Williams doorstep with his bloodied son, Jack Williams had turned him away. "My son says he took no part in this escapade. I suggest you and your family just forget all about this unfortunate incident."

After Sam was born, David had grimly insisted on erasing both Judaism and Christianity from their lives in order to protect his only child from the persecution he suffered.

It wasn't until Sam had finished high school and was contemplating police work as a vocation that Grandfather Benjamin told him the ugly truth about his grown son's painful childhood, as well as its consequences. Tears rolling down his face as he unabashedly held his grandfather to him, Sam vowed to reclaim Judaism and do his best to rid the world of hate and dishonesty, at least in his little town.

While attending the police academy in Springfield, Sam met Addie, a file clerk for the admissions office. Prior to graduation, Sheriff Lloyd Tanner had called Sam in response to his application for deputy sheriff and offered him the job. Although Sam saw the offer as a painless method of assuaging the town's collective guilt, he quickly accepted the position, his head filled with images of Clint Eastwood.

Sam and Addie married under the Chupa and tasted from

the glass of sweet wine. They bought a two-bedroom house three blocks from where Sam grew up, and concentrated on starting a family.

Over the years, Sam's idealistic visions of police work remained vibrant red, while Lloyd Tanner's ethics had gone the way of quicksand. Coasting toward retirement, Tanner's brand of law enforcement depended on the family names of the bad guys involved.

Sam pulled up to the Williams' three-story white frame house with the white picket fence enclosing the tiny front yard. Even the two acres of rolling land that sprawled beyond the house in unrestrained confidence, smattered with frost tip grass, failed to lighten the deputy's mood. He felt no retribution in bearing this death message, only a deep fury for the man who, through years of physical and sexual bullying, finally forced his only daughter to flee.

Mary Jean Williams was drying the last few dinner dishes when the door buzzer sounded. Smoothing her apron and poking a loose strand of graying hair behind one ear, she hurried through the living room where John Paul reclined on a maroon corduroy La-Z-Boy, stroking an oversized tomcat with one hand while he scrutinized The Daily Examiner.

"Sam, this is a surprise," Mary Jean said, shooing the young deputy into the room made cozy through the warmth of the fireplace. "Everything all right with Addie and the baby?"

"We're all just fine, Mary Jean. Thanks for inquirin'. Actually, I'm here on official business."

"Then I'll just leave you two men alone," said Mary Jean, turning back toward the kitchen.

"Actually, this business concerns the two of you. You'd best stay, if I ain't taking you away from something more urgent," said Sam, immediately regretting the irony of his words.

John Paul looked up from his paper. "We both had a long day at work, Sam, and you know we don't take kindly to being disturbed at night. What's so important it couldn't wait until tomorrow?"

"Do you know where Violet is?" Sam blurted.

"She been stayin' down in Peoria with my sister since graduation, working as a file clerk for some granary, but that's old news," said John, waving his hands impatiently.

"When's the last time you talked to her?" asked Sam.

"Couple weeks ago. She called to say she was in a bit of a bind and asked us to loan her some money," said John. Mary Jean sat on the couch, her eyes cast down, knitting needles rapidly clicking back and forth.

"Did she say why she needed the money?"

"Can't say that she did."

"Matt Sawyer been by, asking for her?"

"They broke up awhile back."

"Folks say Matt was fixin' to ask Violet to marry him."

"Look, Sam, we don't appreciate people poking their noses where they don't belong, if you catch my drift," said John, his voice as sharp as the lid on a tuna fish can. "Stop chasing your tail and just get on with it."

"A pregnant teenager was killed ten days ago in a hit-and-run accident in Chicago," said Sam.

"That's mighty unfortunate, Sam, but what does that have to do with us?"

Sam silently handed him the carbon-copied photograph. The abuser's face turned pale as his eyes locked onto the fractured skull. A dreamlike stare followed, the paper slipping from his hands. Sam worked at keeping his balled fists at his side instead of in the store owner's face. Probably tasting his daughter's sweet lips one last time.

The fax paper floated to the floor as gently as a snowflake.

Stretching out one hand, Mary Jean grasped the photograph. "Ah!" she screamed, dropping the paper like burning firewood and fleeing from the room.

"This picture does resemble our Violet, but it can't be her," he sniffled, staring Sam in the eye. "I'll even call my sister right now and prove it to you."

The deputy watched as John Paul, turning his back on him, picked up the black antique style telephone and dialed a seven-digit number, quickly pressing the disconnect. "Hello, Lilly. I was just checkin' up on Vi. Gone to sleep early because she ain't feeling well? Fine. Now you take good care of our girl and yourself, too, you hear?" John Paul hung up the receiver.

"Satisfied?" he said, turning to Sam.

"Any chance I might talk to her myself tomorrow morning?" asked Sam.

"You got a hell of a lot of nerve, scaring my wife and me like this and then having the balls to ask to talk to my daughter. You Jews are all alike, always digging up trouble. You gonna be looking for another job when Lloyd hears what you done. Now get out of here and leave us alone."

Lumbering down the wooden steps, Sam pondered William's chameleon change of attitude, coupled with the bizarre phone call. A sickening thought coursed through his brain. What if Violet ran off because Williams was her baby's father? Glancing back at the house, Sam saw Williams peering back at him as he grabbed a yardstick, then yanked the downstairs curtains closed. Sam shuddered to guess on whom the yardstick would be used.

* * *

Sheriff Lloyd Tanner was already at his desk Monday morning when Sam swung open the door. Catching Sam's look of surprise, Lloyd said, "Lucy's down with the flu and I needed to catch up on a few loose ends, so I came in early. What's your excuse?"

Having tossed and turned all weekend, Sam had intended to telephone the Chicago Police Department and update them on the "Violet" case before the sheriff had a chance to put his spin on the situation, but it was too late now.

"Three of Tom Miller's chickens were poisoned over the weekend. Catch any trout this trip?"

"I didn't do too bad, but I heard you caught yourself a sea tuna and had to let it go."

After three years as deputy sheriff, Sam was used to his boss's use of fish analogies when discussing a crime. "Lloyd, the girl in that picture is Violet Williams, I'm sure of it. See for yourself," said Sam, rummaging through his pocket for the folded fax and handing it to the sheriff.

Lloyd glanced at the photo. "No question about it," he said, crumpling the paper into a ball and stuffing it into his pants pocket.

"What are you doin?" asked Sam.

"Sharks are the king of the sea. Unprovoked, they keep to themselves, not harming the other fish except for food. But once they smell blood, they turn into deadly predators. A human being could get torn to shreds if he ventured out where he shouldn't go."

"Are you saying we shouldn't reveal Violet's identification to the police?" Sam asked incredulously.

"The thing about sharks is, when you slit open their

stomachs, a bunch of smaller fish fall out that you never expected to be there."

"But you're the one who always wants to help the FBI."

"The CPD ain't the FBI, and the Williams ain't murderers. John Paul must have a damn good reason not to acknowledge the death of his only daughter, but that's his business. We don't need to have our town's name smeared all over the newspapers."

"I wouldn't want to be a party to obstructing justice."

"In this economy, Sam, it's mighty hard to act all high and mighty, especially with a wife and new baby depending on you."

"I need some time to think," said Sam, marching out the door.

Watching Sam briskly walk toward the coffee shop, his head down against the snow flurries, Lloyd punched four, the Williams' telephone code, wiping imaginary dust off the new beige telephone they bought him two years ago at Christmas.

"John? Lloyd here. You won't have no problem with Sam."

Chapter Twelve

Beth sprinkled a handful of rose-scented bath salts into a yellow plastic laundry tub and slipped her feet into the warm, soapy water. Thanks to the captain's little medical emergency, she'd been on shift for twenty-four hours straight; no wonder she felt like a handful of used-up tea bags.

Amazing how a person could separate emotion from professional duty, she thought, her toes making tiny waves in the water. After the way he treated her, he deserved a body bag and freezer, not a starched white bed sheet and concerned doctors and nurses. A bolt of guilt rewarded her with a sudden pounding headache. Who was she to judge, she who had taken another woman's child?

Surprisingly, Beth felt little moral discomfort concerning Ruthie. Sue and her foster kids doted on the infant, and lately, Auntie Beth spent more time at Sue's house than in her own home. Dust bunnies floating in the sunlight above her living room sofa attested to her benign neglect.

But there was no way Beth could exorcise the images of a young mother left to die, her blood slowly draining into a nearby sewer.

Swishing her feet around in the luke-warm water one last time, she reached for the foot-cream and towel, breathing a sigh of relief that Angie was finally out of the picture. Life was so unpredictable. If the paramedic officer had not shirked her responsibility, Baby Ruthie might be nursing at her mother's breast this very moment.Even to her own ears, that accusation rang false. Angie had been correct; hemorrhaging through the ears was a death sentence. The mother would never have made it. Yet Angie had been so cold blooded about refusing the young mother her invaluable expertise. Those initial feelings of panic and fury once again threatened to overtake her, but Beth focused on re-claiming her breathing. With no one else alive who'd witnessed the accident, her guilt and fears could finally take a permanent siesta.

Leaning against the unmarked Chevy, Maggie flicked a stick of peppermint chewing gum into her mouth and continued to wait for Paddy to appear. She checked her Roledex for the fifth time in ten minutes. In the five years he'd been her boss, she remembered the numerous admonishments she had received when even sixty seconds past roll call. But since retiring last summer, former police chief Paddy O'Callahan seemed to have switched to Eastern Standard in a Central Standard time zone.

She really shouldn't complain. The white haired gentle giant had been like a father to her, mentoring her through the police academy, then, upon recognizing her talents in analyzing and persistence, promoting her to detective. So when Paddy's long-time friend had requested Paddy's presence following a near-fatal heart attack, she had quickly ordered Paddy to set aside the pelican he was whittling and hop into the passenger side. He'd gone inside to clean up and tell Sara, his wife of fifty years, that he was going out.

The slam of the passenger door signaled Paddy's arrival. "Hey, thanks for driving." he beamed, slowly settling his muscular body into the leather seat. "Head north on Central."

"Yes, sir," Maggie smiled back, steering out into traffic. "Your friend's been out of the hospital about three weeks now, right?"

"Yeah," Paddy shuddered. "Still gives me the creeps seeing Julian lying in intensive care, hooked up to IVs, pee bag, and heart monitor. He looked real fragile underneath those starched white sheets."

"Gossip around the station says only one firefighter and the fire department chaplain on his crew set foot at the hospital."

"So he's not the most popular guy in town. Anyway, the assistant fire house chief rang up the nurses' station every day to check on Julian's progress, and the Sauganash Garden Club sent a bouquet of azaleas."

"Must be rough having so many of your old cronies pass away."

Paddy sighed. "They're dwindling as fast as five cases of Bushmill's Whisky in the hands of a snow crew twenty-four hours after plowing out the city."

"Rumor has it that several years ago, your friend's fire engine rolled over two small kids playing in the street. He was drunk at the time, right?"

"Just let sleeping dogs lie. That's why I never introduced you to the guy."

"Sorry," Maggie mumbled. "Just making conversation."

Uncle Paddy had been far from a saint during his thirty-five years on the CPD, looking the other way as his police buddies shook down small business owners whose monetary contributions enabled them to drive Cadillacs and send their kids to Ivy League colleges. He'd once shared his philosophy with her over an empty shot glass line-up of Irish Whiskey. "With the salary cops are paid to daily confront drug dealers, hustlers, and wackos, they deserve a bonus."

Paddy had enjoyed a cushy job as deputy police chief of special services, arranging traffic control and security, designing parade routes, and mapping out crime prevention positions for special events. The den walls boasted nearly two dozen eight by ten inch parade pictures of Paddy escorting visiting federal officials as well as six mayors and three governors. He even got to meet Pope Paul on a visit to Chicago. His only regret was that he'd failed to foresee the consequences of the '68 Democratic Convention.

But some guardian angel had flapped away the pockmarks of Paddy's dance with corruption, and six-months ago, he had sailed into retirement with a clean file.

At first, retirement had seemed a blessing. But the quiet and sameness of each day were plucking the color from his life like so many peacock feathers. Sarah was already pressing him to make some travel plans for them. Damn. She still needed to talk to her godmother about getting fitted with a new hearing-aid.

"Time's just floating by," Paddy commented, easing his tall frame out of the car. Maggie stood silently at his side while Paddy knocked sharply on the door of the tan brick Georgian.

Before her uncle's fist had banged the knocker a second time, a young blond boy, about fifteen-years-old, gently opened the door.

"Follow me," the boy said softly, turning towards the back of the house.

Although it was only 4:00 p.m., the drapes were tightly drawn throughout the house, projecting a mausoleum affect. Accompanying Paddy and the boy down the darkened hallway, Maggie noticed a light coming from a bedroom. Bowing, the boy quietly opened the door, then left them to their visit.

Julian Paine sat propped up in bed against two oversized pillows, his silk emerald-green lounging pajamas slightly rumpled.

"How you feeling, Jules?" asked Paddy, carefully settling his big frame into the fragile-looking white wicker chair next to the blond wooden bed frame.

"Could be better," answered Julian, his eyes dull with pain.

"Your chest still hurting?"

"Only when I move," laughed Julian, weakly.

"Well, it takes awhile to recover from a heart attack. Remember Joe Cogliono down at the Seventh Precinct? The guy was only in his early fifties when he dropped dead from a stroke 'cause he went back too soon."

"Uncle Paddy, your friend doesn't want to hear that!"

Finally her uncle acknowledge her presence. "This is my godchild, Maggie O'Connor. She's a major accidents investigator with the CPD."

Paine glanced at her. "Pleased to meet you. Hey Paddy, where you been keeping this little beauty?"

"She only came on board five years ago. You and I haven't seen each other for a long time."

"I know, it's my fault. Don't worry about it. Listen, I need some help."

"Name it."

"Remember reading about a hit-and-run on the West Side last Thanksgiving?"

"That the case where a white teenager gave birth and the baby disappeared?"

"That's the one. Where are the police with this investigation?"

"Mind telling us why you're so interested?" asked Maggie, her antennae up.

Paine glanced at Maggie, then back at Paddy. "Am I correct to assume that whatever goes down in here is private?"

"Understood," Paddy answered quickly, silencing his godchild with a look she knew so well. "What exactly are we looking for?"

"Has anybody been charged in the accident? Was the baby ever found?"

"Okay pal, let's see what we can find out."

"Look, I know I haven't been the greatest pal to you over the last three decades, but I intend to change all that," said Julian, looking at Paddy.

"Promises, promises," joked Paddy, patting his friend on the arm. "You get some rest now."

The young boy reappeared from nowhere to escort Maggie and her uncle out.

"Hey, I didn't appreciate you shutting me out in there," said Maggie.

"You women are so sensitive," said Uncle Paddy, rolling his eyes.

"Anyway, something about your buddy smells mighty nasty. You came out of the wash and into retirement squeaky clean. Don't jeopardize your reputation over this scum bag."

"Actually, I thought you might want to throw yourself in the ringer this time."

"You're kidding, right? I refuse to get involved in any dirty stuff."

"I'm disappointed that you would even think I'm asking you to cross the line. Look, you can see the guy is in bad physical condition. Just research the answer and pass it along to me."

"Fine, but if it turns out that he is a witness or a suspect in this case, I'll come down on him like a hurricane."

"Agreed."

Maggie opened the car door for Paddy. "That's enough excitement for one day."

Chapter Thirteen

Carefully positioning himself on a wooden folding chair opposite the captain's frozen English garden, RJ balanced a Styrofoam cup of coffee on his knees.

"It's hard to believe that paine-in-the-ass has already been out two months," said the firefighter, grimacing as a few drops of hot liquid splattered his lap. "By the time he comes back, his garden will probably be thawed."

"Don't get too cocky. He's supposed to be back from sick leave next week. I can't wait to see what new tricks the well-rested captain will pull," said Beth, hugging herself more in trepidation than against the cold morning wind.

"Hey, you've got nothing to worry about anymore. You saved the Paine's life."

"Somehow I don't think that's going to make a bit of difference as far as the love and respect the captain has for me," said Beth, sipping her green tea.

"So he hates women. Look how he treated Angie. Didn't even attend her cremation."

Beth felt her cheeks turn crimson. She'd been so involved with Baby Ruthie, the funeral had completely slipped her mind.

"Anywho, you can't take that shit personally. Did Wally ever tell you about the time he found a 'kiddie porn' magazine underneath Paine's desk when he was on clean-up duty?"

"I can believe it."

"Had some real nasty pictures in it. The Cap must be a subscriber because the cover had his home address. Probably brought the magazine to the fire house so he could jerk off between alarms."

"Did I ever tell you your mouth is like a drainage pump?" Carefully balancing the coffee cup on one knee, RJ grinned. "Just let the crap roll off you."

"Advice taken," said Beth, managing a grin. Inside, she still anxiously wondered what surprises Paine had in store for her.

Eric poured some lemon zinger herb tea from the miniature teapot and passed it across the bare wood table to Beth. "So what made you decide to finally go out with me?" he asked, leaning forward.

Beth breathed in the sweet aroma before taking a sip. "I guess I was curious why you still asked me out even though I gave you the total brush-off at Sue's party."

"I gather you like guessing games."

"Not particularly. It's just that I've been so distracted lately." At the next table, two college kids were engaging in a serious game of chess.

"Anything you'd care to share?" asked Eric. "My art-history students cling to my every insight."

Beth momentarily appraised his face. All she saw staring back was his concern for her. "Say you found a priceless Renoir hidden in an abandoned warehouse replete with rodent droppings and spider webs. Would you deliver your prized possession to the nearest art museum, knowing that the art piece would float from art museum to art museum around the world, or would you tote your newest treasure home and hang it on an empty wall so that only you might enjoy its merits?"

"Wait a minute. Is that actually your dilemma?"

Smiling, Beth shook her head.

"Well that's a relief," said Eric, laughing. "I guess I would do the right thing and bring the painting to the nearest art museum."

"Ah," said Beth.

"What would you do?"

"If the art piece was going to be toted all over creation, never enjoying a permanent home, I'd have to seriously consider the alternative."

"Why did you ask?"

"I just wanted to see how your mind works," she said.

"Like I said before, you enjoy playing games. So how do you know Sue?" he asked.

"We met the first day of high school. She'd just moved here from North Carolina and looked so forlorn sitting in general science, like a kitten caught on a roller coaster," smiled Beth, caressing one arm with her other hand as she remembered.

"And you rescued her from the clutches of loneliness?" asked Eric, leaning back in his chair.

"I rescued her, but not with that motivation in mind. Being

the only child of two professors, I hung around libraries, art museums, and music recital halls a lot. The kids at school thought I was a nerd."

"So you saw another vulnerable kid and latched on?"

Beth nodded, taking another sip of tea. The classical music had stopped and the coffee house was quiet except for mumbled voices.

"Somehow I sensed that my alter-ego hid beneath her loneliness," Beth said. "Even at fourteen, she was polite while I was all sharp edges. She was sweet and thoughtful, more interested in listening to my adolescent insecurities than studying for exams, while I would sail through advanced chemistry, then cut class after lunch to attend a free university lecture on the relationship between allopathic and homeopathic medicine. By junior year, my parents had finally caught on to my frequent class disappearances. They transferred me to Our Lady of Lourdes where the nuns wore habits. Actually, their methods of teaching were far more experimental and exciting."

"What happened to your relationship once you attended different schools?"

"Every night we'd get on the phone. I'd talk. She'd listen."

Eric smiled. "Sounds like she's got an intuitive knack for giving people what they need."

"What about you? How do you know Sue?"

"Shortly after her husband died, she signed up for an Introduction to Art History course I was teaching at the junior college. Sometimes after class, we'd discuss Rembrandt and Monet over a quick cup of coffee. We became good friends over the years."

"I'm surprised she never introduced us before," said Beth.

"Probably because I was married."

Beth's heart dropped. "You're married?"

"Was. After eleven years, my wife left me for her best friend. Both women were well-respected tax attorneys at a conservative downtown firm but when the senior partners found out about their liaison, they booted them out. When Margaret threatened to sue them for sex discrimination, the president made a few phone calls and was able to secure positions for both of them at a large New York firm. The only stipulation was that they not let on that they're lovers."

"How hypocritical that sexual preference still overshadows job performance," said Beth. "It must have been a shock, though, to have your wife leave you for a woman."

"I think my injured ego would have throbbed more had Margaret run off with another man. Somehow, I understand how she might believe an older woman could provide the nurturing she needed. Frankly, I think it worked out for the best. My wife sucked the last drop of patience from my reservoir, and even she would tell you that my reservoir runs pretty deep. There's no animosity between us and we never had kids. I just hope she finally found happiness."

"I'm not sure I could be that generous if the tables were turned," said Beth.

"Have you ever been married?" asked Eric.

Suddenly Beth felt the pangs of her defeated marriage plans with Michael and the miscarriage that followed. Soon she'd be talking about Ruthie—and she wasn't about to tell that story to another living soul. Then she remembered a particularly juicy TV movie she'd recently seen. Hopefully she could remember it all. "I was married for a few hours once upon a time. On the night of senior prom. I wanted to experience what sex was all about, but as a good Catholic girl, I was scared I'd burn in hell. So I cajoled the jock I was with into marrying me."

"How did you pull that one off?" laughed Eric.

"I promised my dad would get him into the University of Chicago's sports Department of Medicine. I didn't know if such a department even existed, but Roger bought the idea so we did. Get married, that is."

"You really go after what you want. Did the marriage match your expectations?"

Beth laughed. "Not exactly. We eloped and got married at the Cook County courthouse. Roger was gulping down Budweiser Lite. He fell asleep on the horn, and I grabbed the wheel. I didn't even know how to drive, so we were swerving all over the place until a police car pulled us over. Our car hit a tree. My parents weren't too happy about the whole incident.

"The next day, they had the marriage annulled. That's when I knew God was saving me for the straight and narrow. I decided to become a nun."

"Didn't you say you used to be a medical librarian before you signed up to become a paramedic?"

"Changed my career goals," said Beth, smiling. She looked at her watch. "Listen, I've had a great time, but I can't stay for the music. I've got to be up early."

"But tomorrow's Sunday."

"I work a twenty-four hour shift every three days. Sunday's no exception."

"No problem. I'll drive you home."

"Don't worry about it. I'll catch the bus."

"I don't feel comfortable letting you roam around Hyde Park alone at night."

"You forget—I'm used to the streets. That's my job."

"Can I give you a call?

"I'll be in touch." Grabbing her white wool coat with the purple Van Gogh scarf, she headed out the door.

Shaking his head in admiration, Eric meandered toward the cash register as he muttered, "She sure knows how to paraphrase a movie plot."

Chapter Fourteen

The squad car pulled up in front of the old Chicago Theater. Right off the bat, Maggie noticed the Emerald Society milling around, awaiting their formal assignment for their position in the parade route. Mayor Daley would soon arrive in his black limousine, flanked by his bodyguard and driver.

Emerging from the driver's side, Paddy appeared focused, as if he was still in charge of orchestrating the parade route and keeping bystanders safe. Four uniformed police officers were positioned at each intersection. The major intersections had been roped off from Lake to Van Buren since 8:00 a.m.

Maggie glanced at her watch. The parade wouldn't start for another forty-five minutes, but thousands of people were already lining up along State Street in anticipation.

Although spring was fast approaching, most pedestrians clutched their winter jackets against a cold, gusty wind. Floats of all shapes and sizes adorned the streets, representing a vast assortment of ethnic contingencies. High school marching bands from all over the city lined up in formation, and the Irish Step Dancers rehearsed their folk dances.

They pushed their way through hordes of people. "How does it feel to not have to be responsible for insuring the safety of visiting dignitaries walking in the parade?" Maggie shouted over the din.

Paddy gave her a thumbs-up sign, then waved to several beat cops.

Following Paddy towards the step-off point, Maggie felt a pat on her lower back. Maggie whirled around.

"How's retirement treating your godfather?"

Maggie smiled, remembering Elf, the little guy who'd once saved Paddy's life. "Ask him yourself; he's right up ahead." Just as she was about to continue through the crowd, she remembered. "Hey Elf, you got a minute?"

"Sure," said the lieutenant, glancing down at his roster to verify his officers' assigned posts. "What's going on?"

"You remember that hit-and-run case last November where a pregnant teenager gave birth but the baby was never found?"

"That story rings a bell. Happened just before Thanksgiving. What about it?"

"Have you guys gotten any tips on the missing baby?"

"Why you asking?"

"I'm not at liberty to say. Can you look into the situation and get back to me?"

"What are friends for?" The *Elf* smiled as he was waved over by the deputy in charge of the parade. "Give my regards to Paddy."

"Sure thing," said Maggie, hurrying to catch up with her uncle.

Spotting him through the crowd, she grinned. He'd donned

a green sequined derby and was flipping it through the air, to the laughter of his old cronies. Hopefully he'd not misplaced his trust in her.

"Hey, Uncle Paddy," Maggie called, as she and Monroe sauntered up the driveway lined with bird sculptures "Looking good."

There came a familiar chuckle from deep inside the garage. "What, me or the pelican?"

"Both." Maggie glanced at the hummingbird Paddy was sanding. "We just thought we'd stop by and say hello."

"Well, come on into the house, and Sarah will make you both some coffee."

"How 'bout a raincheck? We're on the way back to traffic headquarters.

"I still can't get over how smoothly the parade went last week. Your new chief was really on his toes. The police presence was terrific."

"We'll tell him. Listen, in reference to Captain Paine's inquiry about that hit-and-run last November, no suspects have been questioned."

"Okay. Thanks for letting me know."

"It's a real mystery, no clues, no leads."

"Thanks for checking it out," said Paddy, looking visibly relieved.

"It might help reopen the case if we could question your friend."

"Look, I don't want to be rude to my best friend's kid and her partner, but I'm going to have to ask you to steer clear of this."

"Don't you wonder why the fire chief is so interested?"

"This subject is closed," said Paddy, turning back to his wooden sculpture.

"See you around Uncle Paddy," said Maggie, as she and Monroe headed back down the driveway to their unmarked Chevy.

Maggie slid back into the passenger's seat. "How 'bout you and I drop in on the fire chief for a chat?"

"It's worth a shot," shrugged Monroe, tossing his clipboard on the dash and turning the ignition.

Chapter Fifteen

It was a bright sunny Sunday afternoon. Beth was humming Mozart's Concerto in F Minor as she sprayed down the three living room windows overlooking the street, then squiggied them dry. Peering out onto the street, she noticed the absence of cars, typical on a spring weekend. University faculty taking in the Museum of Science and Industry or strolling down by the beach. College students had gone home for the weekend.

Her humming ceased as a male figure exited a shiny black Cadillac. Squinting into the sunlight at the numbers on her brownstone, Captain Julian Paine climbed the narrow cement stairs, wincing in pain all the while.

As she watched his laborious ascent, an ominous feeling washed over her. It had only been eight weeks since her fire chief's heart attack; way too soon to attempt a two-minute drive to the grocery store, let alone a thirty-five minute excursion clear across the City.

Back at the firehouse, official word was the Captain had been confined to bed rest and warned against strenuous activity, including stairs. Upon his return to work next week, he was to tackle nothing but paper work.

"Why, Cap, this is a surprise," said Beth, swinging open the front door.

"I wanted to come in person to thank you for taking care of me at the fire house," said Paine ingratiatingly.

Wondering if he remembered her mumbled words as she had lifted him onto the ambulance, Beth smiled tentatively. "No problem."

"I'm a little winded from these stairs," Paine said, smiling disarmingly. "Any chance I can get a cup of coffee?"

"I'm sorry, please come in," said Beth, swinging open the door. "Just lay your coat on the fireside chair, and I'll get you a cup."

Retreating to the kitchen, Beth glanced over her shoulder at her fire captain. His back to her, Paine was fingering around in his pants pocket for a missing item; perhaps one of his many cigars. His other hand smoothed the crocheted table covers adorning the living room end tables. Beth watched as he briskly patted the flowered pillow cushions that decorated the gold velvet couch, then edged past a hard-backed wooden chair with an embroidered seat cover that sat side-by-side with an antique coffee table. He pulled a handkerchief from his shirt pocket and swiped at the dusty leaves on the potted Diffenbacias aligning the windowsill. Poisonous to dogs and cats but obviously not to humans.

Beth unabashedly stared at her fire captain as he brazenly examined each of the framed family photographs sitting atop the parson's table. She stifled a gasp as Paine's eyes rested on a recently taken photograph of her smiling as she cradled a baby in her arms. Of course he must have recognized Sue Dotson, his neighbor, in the photograph; she was leaning over the rocking chair from behind, her eyes shining with joy as she hugged Beth and the baby.

Beth felt her chest tighten with anxiety. Obviously, the Captain noticed the baby was light cocoa in color. Sue was too nonchalantly posed for this baby to be a new addition to her foster care family. But she was just scaring herself, just like she used to do before final exams. There was no way Paine could connect the dots. The only witness to the kidnapping was dead. Maybe she and Angie were both lucky. To the outside world, both their reputations remained intact. Beth breathed in from her diaphragm, then let it out slowly.

"Here you go, Cap. Be careful, it's hot," said Beth, carefully balancing a teal-blue rimmed china cup and saucer as she re-entered the living room.

"You have some lovely furniture here," said Paine, carefully sipping the hot liquid.

"Thanks. My parents were into antiques," said Beth. "So what brings you all the way to Hyde Park from Sauganash?"

"Like I said before, just wanted to say 'thanks' for saving my life back at the firehouse."

Knowing him the way she did, she didn't buy the life-saving story he'd told her at the door. "A phone call would have been just as good."

"Courtesy is always worth the extra effort. These days, parents fail to teach their children the art of good manners. Your own parents died awhile back, didn't they?" the captain asked casually.

Beth nodded. "They were killed in a car wreck. That's when I decided to become a paramedic."

"I, myself, have always questioned why the fire department decided to hire paramedics," Paine said, staring at the steam rising from his cup. "Firemen, sorry, firefighters, have always saved lives."

Beth felt the light red hair on her arms begin to itch. Attempting a neutral tone, she smiled. "We're there to take care of cardiac arrests and gun shot wounds so you guys can concentrate on fighting fires."

"Obviously you've added kidnapping to the list," the Captain hissed through clenched teeth. "Listen, let's stop beating the rag. If you transfer out of my fire house, I won't expose your little secret."

Shocked at his Jekyl/Hyde change in behavior, Beth felt her heart pounding in her ears. Then a surge of indignation shot through her. "Funny you should use the word expose, Cap," Beth spat, her armpits damp against her white velour sweat suit.

"What the hell are you talking about?"

"Everyone knows you keep a secret supply of reading material hidden in your desk!"

"I can suspend you from the department for snooping in my office," Paine bellowed.

"Aren't you the big hypocrite?" Beth yelled back. "How do you think the fire department is going to react to a thirty-five-year veteran who fucks little boys?"

Looming over her, Paine lunged for Beth's throat with both hands, his face the color of ripe watermelon.

Instinctively, Beth pushed the captain away with one swift motion. Breathing hard, she clutched the wing-backed chair, watching him fall backwards in slow motion, his head striking the corner of the antique end table. A ceramic vase of English ivy toppled onto his head.

Beth panicked as the gash on Paine's forehead spurted blood. Had she hit an artery? Reacting as a trained paramedic, she grabbed. several hand towels from the bathroom and pressed them against the captain's wound to stop the blood flow.

Kneeling over him, a glut of emotions flooded her. If he lived, she'd be waitressing at Denny's for eternity, not knowing what would happen to Ruthie. But could she handle yet another person's death on her conscience? Once again, she had to save this bastard's life. Saving the captain would be her retribution. Lacking the proper bandages and equipment to help the captain, she dialed 911.

Beth was still applying pressure to the wound when the doorbell rang. Jumping to her feet, she opened the front door to find one paramedic holding a jump bag and his partner holding a stair chair. Beth recognized the second medic as one she had gone through paramedic training with at Christ Hospital.

"What's up, Beth?" asked Jim Johnson.

"Get in here. He's bleeding."

"Holy shit," said the paramedic, eyeing the blood-soaked rug as he wrestled into a pair of rubber gloves. "What were you guys doing, playing house? Move that table; we need more room."

As Beth pulled the table across the floor, Jim removed the towel from the captain's head, exposing the injury. Opening the jump bag, he quickly tore open three packs of sterile four-by-four bandages. Blood clots converted the captain's silver-white hair into a Bingo card.

Dazed, Beth watched Jim apply a pressure dressing, then wrap a roll of Kerlix around the captain's head to keep the dressing in place. Finally the blood pressure cuff.

Beth's face flushed in anticipation as Jim's partner picked up her information clipboard. How could she answer questions about the captain without nailing her own coffin?

"What's the guy's name?"

"Julian Paine."

"Does he live here?"

"No, he lives on Minnehaha in Sauganash, but I don't know the exact address."

The paramedic officer looked up from the clip chart, her eyebrows raised. "Oh?"

"He's the captain of my fire house. He just came to visit. It was an accident, just an accident," Beth babbled.

Loading the captain like a sack of oranges onto the stair chair, the two paramedics wheeled him down the stairs. Beth followed with the jump bag and clipboard, grateful that most of her neighbors were safely ensconced in their downtown or university offices.

"We better put this guy on a board if we're going over to Billings," said the paramedic officer.

"Right. He might have a neck injury, too," said Jim, snapping the C-collar around the captain's neck, then placing the backboard on the stretcher.

Glad for something to do, Beth placed her foot against the wheel of the gurney and held on. It was a grim reminder of the captain's first heart attack at the firehouse.

Lifting the stretcher into the ambulance, Jim slammed the back door. "You coming with us?"

Beth stood rooted to the ground. "I don't think so."

As the ambulance pulled off, sirens blasting, Beth stumbled back up the stairs to her house. Pushing the front door open, she was immediately overcome by the sweet smell of dry blood clinging to her Oriental Rug.

Dizziness and nausea pummeled her insides. Images of internal affairs investigators overtook her as she fainted.

After the two paramedics transferred the captain from the stretcher to the hospital cot, Jim grabbed some bleach from the supply cabinet and began wiping down the stretcher. His partner replaced the bandages and backboard they had used on the run.

Wheeling the cot into an empty ER room, Martina, the young Filipino nurse, noted that the captain's breathing seemed irregular, finally stopping.

"Doctor!"

Closing the drape around them, the doctor and two nurses began CPR.

Out in the hallway, the paramedics finished packing their supplies. Listening to the hoopla as they headed out the door, the paramedic officer handed Jim a red book. "Hey Jim, pack this with the patient's personal belongings, will ya?"

"Sure thing," said Jim, eyeing the cover. It was a red diary and it was unlocked.

Liaison officer Frank Martino was scrutinizing the pathologist report concerning a three-year-old victim who had fallen through the window of his ninth floor Cabrini Green apartment when the phone rang.

"Martino here," he barked into the mouthpiece.

A heavily-accented voice greeted him on the other end. "Detective Martino, this is Dr. Saki from Billings Hospital Emergency. I thought you should know that ME 93-602, currently being transferred to the morgue, involves the death of a Chicago fire captain who had been visiting one of his paramedics in her home when nine-one-one was called."

"Thanks for the tip," Martino said politely, then slam-dunked the receiver. "Never a moment's peace around here," he muttered to himself, turning back to the pre-school child's file.

An hour later, his receptionist stuck her head through the door. "Sorry to bother you, sir, but I found this note on fatal case number 93-602 as I was putting together his personal effects and I thought you might want to see it."

Grunting, the detective unfolded the note, which looked as though it had been torn from a diary, and ran his eyes down the contents. He checked the case number the clerk had brought him, then the number the ER doc had called on. "It's a match!"

Placing the three-year-old's file in his *to be continued* basket, Martino put in a call to Sergeant Letterman over at Major Accidents.

Sergeant Letterman carefully maneuvered her wheel chair out of her office and into the mastik-floored room occupied by fifteen traffic specialists and detectives working on assorted investigations. Broken water pipes had eaten away the dingy gray flooring and coughs and sneezes echoed through the cold, drafty room. Police officers sat at desks facing each other as they pounded away on typewriters and fired questions into the phone.

Edging her wheelchair up to the traffic specialist division, Letterman held up a fax. "Anybody remember working on a hit-and-run last November involving a homeless woman and a missing baby?"

Looking up from her paperwork, Maggie O'Connor swiveled her chair toward the voice. "Monroe and I were working that case last November. It's been dead for months."

"Not anymore," said the sergeant, handing Maggie the fax and propelling her wheelchair back toward her office.

Maggie skimmed the confession note. "Yes!"

Another police officer swiveled around, his hand over the telephone mouthpiece, frowning.

"Sorry," Maggie mouthed.

"What gives?" asked Monroe.

"News affairs gave us thumbs up on going public with a sketch of the girl!

"What does that have to do with the fax?"

"Evidently a paramedic, possibly stoned on coke, smashed her ambulance into a pregnant homeless girl but never reported the accident because she was afraid of losing her job."

Monroe let out a low whistle through his teeth. "The note say anything about the missing baby?"

"Yeah, but it sounds pretty bizarre. Think I'll go solo and interview the medic."

Chapter Sixteen

Beth was sipping chicken broth and watching an old "Waltons" re-run when a knock reverberated through the heavy oak door. Setting the half-empty bowl on a TV tray and kicking off the white wool blanket, she grabbed a tissue and made her way to the door.

Glancing out the living room window into the late afternoon sun, she noticed a white Chevy parked in front of her house but missed the municipal license plate on the car.

"Hello?" she sniffled behind the door.

"Beth Reilly?"

"Yes."

"I'm Investigator O'Connor with the Chicago Police Department. Can I talk to you a minute?"

Beth suddenly felt feverish. "What about?"

"We're investigating a hit-and-run that occurred last November and we have reason to believe that your deceased partner, Angie Ropello, was involved."

"I have nothing to say. Just go away."

"We have a note possibly implicating one or both of you in the hit and run."

"Listen, I'm in no condition to discuss this right now."

"Oh, right, what with your fire captain dying and all," said Maggie, masking her sarcastic words with a touch of concern. "No problem, I'll get back to you in a few days." Slipping her card under the door molding, she headed back down the stairs.

Beth swung open the door and picked up the business card, clutching her robe against the damp air. "Investigator O'Connor?"

Once in the apartment, Maggie headed for the winged-back chair facing the sofa. She noted the wastebasket brimming with used tissues.

"Look, if you're not feeling well, we can talk later."

"Just get on with it, okay?" said Beth, sneezing into a tissue.

"Were you and your partner involved in a hit-and-run last November occurring near Madison and Halsted?"

Confronted by the police investigator, Beth nodded.

"What happened?"

Beth felt herself start to hyperventilate. "Angie slammed the ambulance into something."

"What were you doing when the accident occurred?"

"I was cleaning up in the back of the rig while we were heading back to the firehouse."

"Did either of you get off the ambulance to check for damage?"

"At first Angie thought we'd banged into a cat or a pothole, but then we looked out the side window and saw this woman lying in the street several feet away."

"What happened then?"

"I'd only been on the rig for six weeks, and Angie was frantic that her professional reputation would be destroyed if anyone found out she'd injured a pedestrian."

"That must have been pretty heavy for both of you."

Beth started to weep.

"By the way, do you know if your partner ever drank or did drugs at work?"

"I never actually saw her take drugs or drink at work, but I suspected something was going on because her behavior was often erratic."

"What do you mean 'erratic'?"

"The night of the accident, we'd brought this young trauma victim to the hospital and afterwards, Angie pulled her usual disappearing act."

"Disappearing act?"

"After coming out of the bathroom, she seemed really energized."

"Okay, back to the accident. You guys just took off?"

Beth nodded, sneezing into another tissue.

"Just one more question. Was there any indication that the victim had just given birth?"

Beth felt like fainting; she could taste vomit in her mouth. "I have nothing else to tell you. Please leave," she said, dizzily rising from the sofa.

"Let me give it to you straight. If you know something and refuse to cooperate, we're going to have to go to your superiors and ask your department to start an internal investigation into the circumstances surrounding this woman's death. Thanks for your time."

Beth slammed the door behind the investigator. The detective had caught her with her mental and physical defenses down, when she was too sick to keep mum. The scary thing was that it had felt good to confess. She'd hit the brakes just in time. Running to the toilet, she heaved until only bile remained.

"I've just had a visit from a police investigator; we've got to talk." Beth spoke into the cordless phone as she feebly pushed a sponge-mop over the white ceramic squares covering her bathroom floor.

"What about?" asked Sue Dotson, holding the phone to one ear as she swung open the oven door to check on the meatloaf.

Beth felt a rush of anger. Her best friend was still pretending that nothing criminal had occurred five months ago when she'd agreed to raise Ruthie as her own. "Look, the police know about the hit-and-run. We've got to get together and plan our next step."

Stirring a big iron pot of creamy mashed potatoes with a wooden cooking spoon, her chin holding the telephone receiver in place, Sue said lightly, "I don't know, Beth, you're still contagious and I don't want the kids to get sick —"

"They traced the accident back to me and Angie."

"Ruthie and Paulie were at the doctor's office Monday."

"But, they don't know about the baby, at least not yet."

"Ginny and Joey rack up every cold bug two preschoolers can find."

"God damn it, Sue! I'm talking Baby Ruthie's security and you're talking common cold. What are we going to do?"

Sue raised her voice forcefully. "You have the nerve to invoke God's name, and ask me what to do? You're the one who thrust us into this garden of evil by kidnapping Ruthie and convincing me to raise her for you. You're the one who allowed the baby's mother to hemorrhage to death. You're the one who shrugged off my concern that you were putting the other children's lives at risk. The morning you shoved Baby Ruthie in my arms like a bag of stolen goods, you assured me that you had all the answers."

"I never thought they'd find out, not after Angie OD'd."

"Satan works in strange ways."

"It was so foggy, nobody could have seen me jump off the ambulance to help that girl," Beth moaned. "And even if they did, I could always say it was Angie."

"You've slipped into the devil's grasp."

"Quit the dramatics! I need your help to figure things out."

"Ever since high school, you've used me to bail you out of your little escapades. And I've always gone along. But we're all grown up now, and I can't go along anymore—not when the lives of eight innocent children are involved. When I think of the emotional pain they'll soon be subjected to because of your whim—"

"You took Ruthie in, didn't you? If anything, we share the blame."

Silence permeated the air.

"Maybe I should just stay away for awhile."

"I'll pray for you," Sue said.

The phone clicked softly in Beth's ear. She laid the receiver against her heart. What had she done to deserve such resentment? Since high school, Sue had been the bricks and mortar bolstering up her universe. In return, she showered Sue's life with laughter and adventure, rare *soul* commodities for a girl responsible for providing free daycare for five younger siblings while her mother attended to the needy souls at the church mission.

Had Sue forgotten how she had befriended the new transfer student from North Carolina when the other high school girls sarcastically commented on her southern twang? How she convinced Mrs. Dotson to allow her daughter to try out for cheerleading? How she accompanied Sue to the abortion doctor when she got pregnant with Billy's baby?

Twenty years later, how she risked her life to present Sue with a newborn infant?

Reliving these moments in their relationship, Beth felt a rage similar to the fury she'd experienced toward Angie that fateful night. In both instances, the two people whose help and respect she craved had denied her emotional comfort, abandoning her to fend for herself.

Short lived like before, the fury shrunk away in defeat. Beth crawled back to the couch, her brain in a fog that no amount of Claritan could clear. How could she have so misjudged her best friend? Reaching into her robe pocket, she fingered the rainbow-colored pacifier that she'd bought for Ruthie the day before. As she detached its clear plastic molding, tears rolled down her cheeks. She might never get the chance to deliver the new "pacy." In a split-second, it was in her own mouth.

The telephone's insistent ring jarred her from her frantic thoughts.

"Hi, Beth, this is Eric Saunders. I know you said you'd call me, but hey, it's been two months and a guy could drop dead in the meantime."

"A lot's been going on," Beth said.

"What do you say we grab a veggie-burger and carrot chips?"

"Sounds great, but I should warn you that my cold might be contagious," Beth smiled into the phone, feeling better already. Resolutely tossing the string of used tissues into the wastebasket and shaking out her white wool blanket, she had a hunch that Mr. Art Professor-in-residence might be her ticket out of this mess.

Chapter Seventeen

RJ sat in the tower during his assigned night watch, half-listening to the fire radio for incoming calls and watching David Letterman on a fourteen-inch TV. Outside the cubicle, the firehouse was silent as the other firefighters and paramedics caught some shut-eye in between calls. Staring out the full-length window facing the firehouse parking lot, he saw a white Chevy pull up.

"Anyone here?" called Maggie.

RJ stepped out of the tiny office. "Can I help you?"

The investigator flashed her badge as she quickly walked up the half-flight of stairs. "Police. We're looking into the death of a paramedic by the name of Angie Ropello. She work your shift?"

"You'll have to talk to our commanding officer. He's not available at the moment."

"You guys must be pretty upset, what with your firehouse captain dying."

"It was a shock, but listen, Miss, you should really be talking to someone at headquarters."

"Do you work with a paramedic named Beth Reilly?"

"Occasionally."

"How long has she been on the job?"

"I don't know. She's a candidate—not that long."

"Did you know a paramedic by the name of Angie Ropello?"

"Of course. She was working this house when I was assigned seven years ago."

"Do you have any knowledge of either paramedic doing drugs or drinking on the job?"

"Listen, I really can't answer any more questions."

"Just one more. How did Beth and the captain get along?"

"The captain hated her guts. Hey, you got to leave now. A call's coming in." Without a backward glance, RJ disappeared back into the tower, grabbing a scrap of paper and scribbling the address coming over the speaker while pressing the firehouse bell to alert the crew.

Within thirty seconds of the alarm, a handful of firefighters in stocking feet plunged into heavy black boots neatly aligned along the fire truck, the motor already running, the garage door letting in the cool night air. Sirens flashed as the truck pulled out of the firehouse. No one noticed Maggie as she hurried out the side door.

Deputy Sam Aarons stood in the darkened living-room, absent-mindedly pushing the baby's wind-up swing while he attempted to watch the 5:00 news and wolf down a Sloppy Joe and Coke.

Addie went to a quilting club social and left Sam to baby-sit for six-month-old Rebecca. On the way home from the sheriff's office, he'd stopped for burgers. Mary Jean Williams was wiping down the snack counter when his entrance jangled the bell hanging from the door. Her husband must have frightened her against any further conversation with him regarding their daughter's death because she quickly disappeared into the kitchen. A teenage girl in streaked blond ponytail had hastily packed his order.

Sam knew John Paul beat his wife and kids. But in a small town like Chilicothe, secrets were hard to unknot. The deputy was just about to toss his used paper plate in the trash when he noticed a young woman's picture to the upper right of the newscaster's face.

Adjusting for static, Sam grimaced at the face of Violet Williams.

"Police have been trying to identify a hit and run victim in an accident that occurred last November. If anybody has information about this woman, please contact the Chicago Police Department."

The 19-inch television seemed to flood the living room in white light, casting him as main character in a whodunit he'd been too reticent to follow.

Seeing Violet's face plastered across the television screen after a five-month moratorium, he could no longer look away while the dead girl's father and the sheriff blithely concealed her identity from the Chicago Police Department. He had to do right by his father and grandfather.

God was giving him a second chance, just as he had given Jacob a second chance in the Old Testament. He would shatter those barriers of silence once and for all.

Fumbling through the kitchen drawer for the female police investigator's phone number, Sam stuffed a big piece of homemade chocolate cake in his mouth as a cushion for whatever fate befell him.

It was 6:00 a.m. Zack Hurowitz and Rich Cazione were cruising east on Madison Street when they spotted a spindly looking man in a stocking cap running from a factory, the alarm blasting the Sunday morning silence. Shoving the car doors open, the two beat cops chased him into the alley, finally subduing him.

Pulling the stocking cap off the suspect's head, and searching him for weapons, Zack said, "Well if it isn't old Jer'."

As he handcuffed the suspect, Rich began reading him the Miranda, "You have the right to remain si—"

"Hey, jerk-head, I know that crap by heart."

"Keep your trap shut unless you're asked to open it, you little shit," said Rich, pushing him into the back seat.

Zack swung open the driver's side and plopped into the front seat. "The back door was open but no signs of forced entry."

"What were you doing in the factory?" asked Officer Cazione.

"I'm paid to come in and clean it up."

"Why'd the alarm go off, Jerr?" asked Hurowitz, turning to face them in the back seat.

"I was going to work and the door was locked so I shifted the door to try to get in. That must have set the alarm off."

"Owner give you a key?"

"O'course."

"You might want to rethink that answer, Jer. Sundays are no-clean days"

"No way."

"The alarm would be on. Just sit tight. As soon as we call your boss and get this thing shut off, we're out of here."

Upstairs at the 12th district station, Hurowitz clamped the suspect's handcuffs onto the D-Ring hanging from the wall, effectively preventing his escape from a window covered with metal gratings and bolted shut. Drawing up a chair, he gently pushed the suspect into it. Cazione noisily pecked out his report on the old Royal typewriter.

They waited for the state's attorney in a windowless room decorated in dingy green and laden with stale smoke; the only color in the room coming from a garbage can belching at its seams with empty food wrappers, pop cans, and old police reports.

State's attorney Charles Egan heaved his solid frame into the narrow wooden chair. "What's up?"

"The suspect was found running from the scene of a possible burglary. His employer at Lobb Wholesaling said he wasn't scheduled to work today."

Egan scanned the report. "Jerry Jablonski."

"It's his third strike in two years."

"He take anything?"

Hurowitz shook his head. "We apprehended the suspect as he fled down the street."

Turning to the suspect, Egan took off his black-rimmed glasses and pulled a tissue from his pocket, wiping unseen smudges from the eyepiece.

"It says here you've been arrested on two previous occasions for burglary, Mr. Jablonski. We're charging you with criminal trespass to property; usual sentence is ninety days at Cook County. Do you want to speak to an attorney?"

"Listen, I don't need no attorney. I'm not going back into that pit. I got some information you might want."

"Don't humiliate yourself by attempting to plea bargain with me, Mr. Jablonski. This is your third offense. You're going down."

"Too bad. Remember that accident on Madison and Green a few days before Thanksgiving?"

"Accidents happen every day in the Windy City, Mr. Jablonski."

"How 'bout a hit-and-run where an ambulance hits a lady?"

"What are you talking about?"

"Will you convince the judge to make nice?"

"Would you prefer I nail you for obstruction of justice?"

"All right, all right. It was early Monday morning, foggy as hell. I was shaking out my dust mop, when I saw this ambulance bang into this lady. She flew into the air like a bag of marbles, then hit the ground with a bang."

Holding his palm up to silence the janitor, Egan turned to Hurowitz. "Contact Major Accidents."

"In all that fog, Mr. Jablonski, how could you determine whether the vehicle was an ambulance or a van?" Maggie asked, as she continued to jot down notes on her yellow legal pad.

"It had a big number all lit up on it."

"Then what happened?"

"This woman gets out the back of the ambulance and goes

over to the lady. She stoops down there for a long time. Then she gets up. She's holding something in her arms. Then the ambulance turns off its lights and splits, leaving the lady lying in the street."

"Can you describe the item that the subject took from the victim before returning to the ambulance?" asked Maggie.

"It looked like a white blanket or sheet or flag."

"How could you tell?"

"'Cause it reflected off a street lamp when the woman ran back to the ambulance."

"This woman who picked up the object on the ground, what did she look like?"

"White, about hundred-thirty pounds, and short, brownish red hair."

"What did you do after you saw them drive off?"

"Went back into the factory, finished my work, and went home."

"All right," said the States Attorney. "We're gonna hold you for twenty-four hours to verify your story. If it pans out, we'll be back to talk to you. Do you remember the number on that ambulance?"

"Sixty"

"Are you sure?" asked Maggie. "Thanksgiving was five months ago."

"Sure I'm sure. My old man's 60th birthday was November 22nd, the same day the accident happened."

"Do you think you could identify this woman from a photo line-up?"

"No problem."

"Your story best be right on the mark or I'll shove your ass right into the lock-up," said Egan.

"Hey, I aim to please."

Chapter Eighteen

"What a bummer. I'm down with the flu for two stinkin' nights and you get all the action on that hit-and-run/kidnapping."

"Get over it, Monroe."

"You think this Beth Reilly is the same paramedic seen by Jablonski?"

"She seemed awfully nervous when I interviewed her. Then again, I'd be pretty unhinged if my captain and partner both croaked within two months of each other. Then there's the confession note."

"So what goes?"

"Reilly says her partner smashed their ambulance into this homeless girl; then they fled the scene without getting off the rig."

"Two paramedics take off, leaving a young woman to hemorrhage to death in the streets? That doesn't jive."

"And the weird thing is, neither of them called for an assist. Supposedly, Angie was afraid of going down on a drug charge, and Beth had only been with the department for six weeks."

"The paramedic must be bullshitting."

"Angie's note said Beth threatened her to keep quiet about the accident and the kidnapping. What's even more bizarre is, last night I interviewed RJ Sloan, this firefighter who works with Reilly. He told me the deceased captain hated her guts. Then the liaison officer tells me the captain dropped dead in her living room. But why would a fire captain be paying a social visit on a crew member he despises?"

"You think it's connected — that he found Angie's confession note and Reilly knocked him off when he confronted her with it?"

"It's all circumstantial, but it makes sense, doesn't it? Maybe this guy was from the old school, like Uncle Paddy, and—Oh, no."

"What?"

"Remember when my uncle told us to steer clear of his friend's interest in the case?"

"Yeah, so?"

"Julian Paine was the fire chief at that station. He must have found the note and asked my uncle to verify its contents so he could blackmail Reilly to quit the department."

"Back to the firehouse?"

Maggie smiled grimly. She and Monroe were always on the same wavelength. "Hang on, I just got to check my message box."

"I'll meet you outside," Monroe said, grabbing his raincoat from the closet.

"Yes!" he heard Maggie shout from the office.

Seeing her partner in the doorway, a quizzical expression on his face, Maggie pulled him aside excitedly. "Remember the missing person's sketch we put out on that runaway teenager? Evidently, Channel Nine aired it tonight and a deputy from Chilicothe picked it up."

"Chilicothe. Isn't that one of those small towns in southern Illinois where we faxed the girl's picture a couple of days after the accident?"

"The point is, the guy recognizes her now, says he can make a positive ID. We got an open invite."

"I'm sold. Where you want to start?"

"How 'bout you hit the cornfields and I'll fan the fire house."

"Sounds good, but I got a feeling this invite ain't so open."

"Why?"

"Five months is a long time to RSVP."

"Give the guy a chance, why don't you, before you ground his ass into putty?"

"You turning into vanilla pudding or something?"

"I'm just saying, there could be extenuating circumstances."

"Like the sheriff told him he'd lose his job if he painted a positive ID?"

"Like they say, truth is stranger than fiction."

"Don't worry, I'll be cool. You know I read all those John Gray books. I'm an open, sharing kind of dude."

"Yeah, right."

Even though the lieutenant had given her the go ahead to present the subpoena, Maggie's hands felt clammy as she pushed through the revolving door leading into the old Kraft building and signed in with two police officers.

Walking up the two stairs leading to the first floor, she rehearsed her retort in case anyone gave her flack about obtaining the photo IDs of paramedics Angie Ropella and Beth Reilly. Veering left, she pushed open the door sporting a simple metal sign: Chicago Fire Department.

The long, narrow hallway would have been great for a game of marbles, her favorite childhood game, but this place was no fairy tale heaven. Firefighters and paramedics on sick leave with everything from the flu to a back injury stoically endured the two-hour wait to see the doctor. She briefly wondered if Beth had checked in since she'd been sick.

Maggie recognized the grumpy old firefighter; he'd been stuck on the medical desk forever. She showed him her badge. "I need to speak to the director of personnel."

Upon hearing she had no appointment, he grudgingly directed her to wait in yet another of the file-laden hallways. Frazzled nurses zoomed down the halls, calling the next patient's name, clamping on yet another blood pressure cuff, and directing the patient into one of two examination rooms to again wait for the doctor.

Finally coming to a glass windowed office, Maggie retrieved the subpoena from her pocket and pushed open the personnel director's door just as the grandfatherly gentleman finished issuing directives to his secretary.

The director glanced at the subpoena. "I have to go through my chain of command before I can release anything."

"Well, who else can I talk to?"

"The fire commissioner, room 105 at City Hall."

Thanking him, Maggie grimaced as she headed out the door. At this rate, her whole morning would be shot.

It was nearing lunchtime and City Hall was a rumble of bodies moving up and down the elevators and through the halls. She pushed past the wide glass door to the fire department and stopped at the receptionist's desk.

Maggie flashed her badge. "I've got a subpoena here for some information regarding two of your paramedics. I'd like to speak to the chief paramedic."

In moments, a tall, immaculately dressed black man appeared. Maggie remembered seeing Loren Thomas interviewed by the press on TV; he was well-educated, impressive looking, and an expert at playing the media.

"Come into my office," said Thomas.

"We're investigating a hit-and-run and possible homicide that occurred on Madison and Green, and one of your ambulances, Ambulance 60, was spotted near the scene. I have a subpoena for photo IDs of the two female paramedics who were assigned to the vehicle as well as the journal and run sheets for that ambulance relevant to November twenty-second."

A frown quickly snuffed the light from the chief paramedic's face. Quickly regrouping, he said, "The journal's at the fire house, and if you've got time to hang around, we'll pull the papers from the Records Division. Most of the stuff's on microfiche."

Maggie stifled her surprise. "I heard tell that all docs are housed on the south side."

"That's ancient stuff," Chief Thomas chuckled. "We've got daily journals going back some sixty years."

Incredulous, Maggie visualized the warehouse going up in smoke. "Is it possible to get the photo IDs of deceased paramedic Angie Ropella and paramedic Beth Reilly today?"

"We can have those for you by this afternoon."

"Great. Thanks for your cooperation."

"Hopefully this situation can be resolved quickly. We don't need yet another blemish on the Department."

"I appreciate how you feel."

Chief Paramedic Thomas shut the door behind the investigator and solemnly punched-in the extension to internal affairs.

Maggie stood on the top step of City Hall, gazing down at people lunching around the Picasso, and breathed in the pungent spring aroma. She'd have the necessary documents in no time. Thomas was known for moving fast when it concerned any wrongdoing by his paramedics. Internal affairs would conduct its own investigation alongside that of the Police.

Suddenly, the static from her hand-held police radio was interrupted by the dispatcher's voice: "Badge 73509, return to police headquarters immediately."

Chapter Nineteen

Jean Edgar was the kind of attorney every gun-wielder and Mafia kingpin wanted on his side. In twenty-five years of legal practice, she'd represented them all, no matter their color, creed, or currency.

Leaning back in an oversized black leather chair, she twirled around toward the glass windows that served as backdrop for every little drama entering her office and stared down at the Hancock Center. So close to the shopping ecstasy of Water Tower Place and no time enjoy it. Too busy defending criminals.

Glancing at her personal diary, she noted that a new client would soon be walking through the glass door to her office with a yet another tale of woe. She was becoming as cynical as a late-night talk show host. When had she forsaken the starry eyed vision of justice she'd felt as a young assistant states attorney?

Stuffing the remains of a salami sandwich on rye into her mouth, she swiped at her lips with a napkin. She had just tossed an uneaten apple into the wastebasket when a middle-age woman dressed in a blue uniform swung open the door.

Jean was surprised to see a woman staring back at her. On the telephone, Reverend Luke had introduced the paramedic named "Reilly" over the phone, never mentioning gender.

She quickly sized up the new client: army-green eyes, middle-class, just shy of forty, short, wavy hair the color of a faded poinsettia.

The attorney extended her hand. "Sit down, please."

Beth stood frozen to the spot, engulfed by plush turquoise carpet and designer-papered walls, trying to decide whether to take the well-coifed woman up on her offer or scram. The only reason she was here in the first place was Sue's unexpected phone call the night before.

"Tonight's five o'clock news showed a picture of the unfortunate girl your ambulance banged into. I contacted Reverend Luke for the name of an attorney to represent you. I asked him to find a woman, someone with a sterling legal record and an abundance of empathy. He referred you to a new congregant of his, who happens to be a former states attorney. Her name is Jean Edgar and she's in the Hancock Building. Your appointment's at one o'clock."

"Sue, I really appreciate this and I'm so sorry that—"

"Please don't embarrass yourself, Beth, I'm only doing this for the good of the children. You still need to make your peace with God before you can be saved. I will no longer contact you and I must request that you follow my lead. God bless you."

A wave-shattering click of the telephone assaulted her ear, followed by silence.

* * *

"Paramedic Reilly? Are you all right?" asked Jean now, a note of concern in her tone.

"I'm sorry," said Beth, shivering involuntarily as she quickly took a seat.

Edgar shrugged aside the paramedic's momentary loss of control. "Many clients come in here, haunted by their own private demons. Why do you think you were referred to me?"

"I'm not really sure."

"I understand that you were one of two female paramedics assigned to an ambulance that was involved in a hit-and-run accident and kidnapping last November, and that you are currently being investigated concerning your role in the accident."

"You don't beat around the bush, do you?"

"I always believe in being direct. It appears that the police are aggressively attempting to identify the deceased victim, a young homeless woman."

Beth said nothing.

"I am unable to evaluate your case unless I have your cooperation."

"Case? There must be some mistake. I'm not suing anybody. I only came to see you at the request of a friend," said Beth, abruptly standing and heading for the door.

"Who no longer wishes to remain your friend, correct?"

Beth hesitated.

"You may wish to reconsider whether walking out that door is really in your best interest, Ms. Reilly," said Edgar. "This police investigation won't go away. They'll be pulling in the ropes sooner or later, and by the looks of it, I would guess sooner.

Forgive me for being so blunt, but it's obvious you could benefit from some legal counsel, wouldn't you agree?"

Beth settled back into the leather chair.

"Good, you're a reasonable person," said the attorney, pulling a pocket-size tape recorder from her bottom drawer. "Now, why don't we start with you telling me exactly what happened the night of the accident?"

Closing her eyes, Beth breathed deeply into the visual image. "My paramedic officer and I had just completed a grisly run involving a boy in a motorcycle accident, and we were returning to the fire house, when I felt a thud."

"Your ambulance banged into something?"

"Yes."

"Who was driving the vehicle?"

"Angie."

"How would you describe her behavior directly preceding the accident?"

"She was exuberant about saving that boy's life."

"Did she normally act that way?"

"Only when she was doing cocaine."

"How did you know she was a drug user?"

"Everybody around the fire house knew."

"Did you ever consider reporting her to the department?"

"Not really. She'd never been in an accident before, and she had a great professional reputation. I felt fortunate to be working with someone that knowledgeable."

"How long had you been a paramedic at the time of the accident?"

"Six weeks." Beth saw the surprise in the other woman's eyes. "Mid-life crisis."

"What type of work did you engage in prior to signing on with the fire department?"

"I worked as a medical librarian for the University of Chicago."

"All right," said the attorney. "Let's go back to the night of the accident. You said you heard a thud; the ambulance had banged into something. Did either you or Angie exit the vehicle to check for damages?"

Beth hesitated. If she told the truth, she'd surely be in jeopardy, but if she lied, she'd be taking the devil's path, as Sue had so recently reminded her.

Edgar turned off the recorder. "Look. The only factor in whether I accept you as a new client is whether we can win the case. I don't believe in morally judging my clients' innocence or guilt; that's up to the courts to decide. What I do demand, however, is complete honesty on your part so that I may best plan my legal maneuvers."

Beth trembled as she felt the attorney's scrutiny. What a relief it would be to give this attorney a play-by-play description of the night's events. But her impulsiveness had gotten her into this mess in the first place. She doubted that the attorney had any information regarding Ruthie; when news finally surfaced about the kidnapping, Sue would lose Ruthie and her foster children to DCFS, and she would win an extended overnight pass to Cook County Jail.

"Ms. Reilly, are you all right?" Jean Edgar asked for the second time.

"I'm sorry. I'm still mourning my partner's death. It's hard to say these awful things about her."

The attorney once again pressed the record button. "You were about to tell me whether you or your partner had exited the vehicle."

"As I told the police investigator who came to my home yesterday, we looked out the side window and saw something lying in the street, but Angie was afraid she'd be discharged for operating a vehicle while on drugs."

"So you were aware that this something was actually a someone?"

"Yes," Beth whispered.

"Yet both you and your paramedic officer fled the scene without administering first-aid."

Beth stared down at her hands. "That's right."

The attorney pressed the stop button. "I'm sorry, Ms. Reilly," she said, her words coming out clipped and professional, "but I don't buy your story. As a new paramedic, you must have felt compelled to get out of the ambulance and do your utmost to assist the victim. Until you are able to trust me with your confidences, I am unable to represent you. Good day."

No sooner had Beth risen to her feet than the attorney was on the phone with another client.

Beth noticed she failed to acknowledge her departure.

Maggie briskly entered the firehouse, intent on questioning the firefighters about Beth's relationship with her captain. All quiet up front except for a dispatcher. Waving her badge up at the window, she headed towards the garage. A gruff voice radiated from a room down the hall.

"An investigation is pending, so we need a 'Form 2' from everyone stating the relationship between Captain Paine and Paramedic Reilly."

"What do you mean relationship? Was he fucking her or what?" asked RJ, looking up from the form.

The battalion chief glared at him. "You guys got the whole shift to complete the forms. Think about what you write. We'll be back." Quickly slipping into a darkened classroom, Maggie watched as he stomped out of the firehouse, flanked by the district chief and IAD investigator, as well as the new firehouse captain.

Loud voices echoed from the meeting room.

"Cops been snooping around here lately. Reilly must be in some deep shit," said RJ, turning back to the other guys.

"How 'bout the top brass in here today?" asked Don, flipping through the packet of questions.

"Exactly," said RJ, attempting to erase several misspelled words on his pencil-smudged paper.

"How much do you guys think we should let on about her and Paine?" asked Don, drumming his pencil on the table.

"I'm putting down that he was always picking on her. Creating a hostile work environment," said Wally, busily scratching away on the form.

"Those sure are five-dollar words, Wall," teased RJ. "You guys remember the time the Cap tossed that menstrual pad across the breakfast table? Donny almost barfed."

Don turned bright red.

R.J. sneered. "The perv used to sneak into the girls' lockers when he thought no one was looking."

"How 'bout the kiddie porn magazines?" Wally interjected. "You'd think a thirty-five year veteran would have enough smarts to keep that stuff locked up."

"One night about 3:00 a.m., he falls asleep in his office and I go in to turn off the TV," added Quinn. "He's got on a home movie of three teenaged boys engaging in sex on this white silk living room couch covered with plastic."

"Ouch!" said R.J.

"You can hear his voice on the video, directing one kid to pee on his white fur rug, wipe it off with a pink kitchen sponge, then squeeze the sponge between his thighs as he deposits it in a bathroom waste basket brimming with cigar butts."

"A fuckin' obstacle course," said RJ.

"Another scene is staged with tropical plants—"

'The Cap does like his plants," Wally cut in.

"—as a backdrop for sex between the boys and an older teenager who speaks no English."

"Paine's been a queer all along!" yells R.J.

"How come you never mentioned this video before?" asked Don, looking up from his writing.

"'Cause I'm mentioning it now," frowned Quinn. "Anyway, at the end of this video, he hands his 'three muskrats' some bills and a pack of baby wipes."

"Cap always said cleanliness was next to godliness," says Wally."

"Look," said Don quietly. "The guy's dead, along with his indiscretions."

"You guys realize that Angie and Paine both died since Beth came on board," said Wally.

"Actually, Beth was the one who revived him two heart attacks ago," Don reminded them.

"Well, now he's dead. Whatever happens, she's on her own," said RJ, underlining his last essay answer with a flourish.

Maggie smiled to herself as she exited the firehouse through the garage. Guess I got all the answers I came for.

* * *

Maggie forced herself to stop fidgeting as she sat facing her lieutenant. "I've got a message from Monroe, says the deputy sheriff in Chilicothe positively ID'd the deceased hit-and-run victim as a pregnant eighteen-year-old named Violet Williams. When she was eight and a half months pregnant, the girl hopped a Greyhound bus to Chicago where she took refuge in a homeless shelter on west Madison. A few days later, she was found dead in the street."

"What about the baby?"

"The medical examiner said the girl probably hemorrhaged to death after giving birth because the placenta was still intact, but the baby was never found."

"What's the connection with your female paramedic?"

"A midnight shift factory worker was shaking out his dust mop when he saw a Chicago Fire Department ambulance hit the girl."

"Maggie, you know we can't issue a warrant just on hearsay. How do you know it was her ambulance he saw?"

Maggie attempted to curb her impatience. "Even though there was a heavy fog the morning of the accident, he was able to make out a neon 'sixty' on the side of the ambulance. Beth Reilly was the paramedic candidate on that ambulance."

"Didn't I hear you say earlier that the driver was also a female paramedic?"

Maggie nodded. "An Angie Ropella. Most likely the one operating the vehicle when it hit the girl. Reilly says neither she nor her paramedic officer exited the ambulance to assist the girl, but this day worker insists he saw one of them jump off the ambulance and go to her."

"Why didn't your guy report this five months ago when the accident occurred?"

"Guy didn't want to get involved then. But he was recently arrested for his third breaking-and-entering. He's doing this for a plea-bargain."

"And he positively identified Reilly as the paramedic who examined the victim?"

Maggie nodded. "Says he saw her pick up something in a blanket—possibly the baby—and get back on the ambulance, leaving the girl lying in the street."

"Are you sure it wasn't the paramedic officer who got off the ambulance to assist?"

"The guy says the paramedic hopped back into the passenger side when she was through examining the girl."

"So Reilly took the baby."

"It sure looks that way from Ropella's confession note. What's even more bizarre is that the firehouse captain had that note safely tucked away in his pants pocket when he was found dead in Reilly's house, supposedly of a heart attack. He could have been trying to blackmail her to quit the fire department when she let on that she'd report his kiddie porn habit."

"Good work, kid. Go for it."

Chapter Twenty

Clutching her health records, Beth searched the unfamiliar halls for the door marked MEDICAL. She'd been through these doors five months ago for her initial physical, but after her flu bug finally bit the dust, she needed to be examined before receiving permission to return to active duty.

Signing in with the receptionist, she slid into a vacant seat at the end of a long line of paramedics patiently waiting for medical attention. She stared off into space, not even pretending to fiddle with her papers. Jean Edgar had really jarred her. Who the heck did she think she was, her warden? She didn't need an attorney anyway. Angie and Paine were history, and Sue would never betray her. All she wanted to do was get back to work and put this kidnapping thing behind her.

"Beth Reilly?" The receptionist's brought her back to reality. "Please step this way."

Beth followed the receptionist down the hall, wondering why

she'd been called before the others. With a sinking feeling, she trailed the receptionist down hall after hall, devoid of patients.

"Excuse me, but I think we've gone a bit too far," she volunteered nervously.

And then the bold gold lettering: "Internal Affairs Division" and fire department brass blocking her way, flanked by a police officer and the investigator who'd interviewed her back at the house. "Ms. Reilly, these two police officers are here to talk to you about a possible criminal matter."

Before she knew what had happened, the officer was saying, "You have the right to remain silent."

"Be careful what you're telling her, that woman is my client," reverberated a voice from down the hall.

Everyone turned to look. Her platinum hair tastefully held back in a bun, high heels clicking down the checkered hall, black leather briefcase swinging at her side, Jean Edgar made her entrance.

Beth did a double take. How could the attorney have known she'd be here? And why was she referring to her as her "client" when she'd just washed her hands of her the day before? Jean gave her a reassuring look.

"IAD will sit in on the questioning to find out if any fire department rules and regulations were broken," continued the fire department supervisor, barely missing a beat.

"I'd like a moment to confer with my client before we begin," said Jean.

"You can use the meeting room over there."

"Thank you." The attorney guided Beth into the interview room, securely closing the glass door behind them.

* * *

"How did you know I'd be here?" asked Beth.

"I've got big friends in small places," chuckled Jean.

"You're probably also curious as to why I reconsidered my decision to represent you."

Beth nodded.

"I've become privy to information you attempted to conceal from me."

Beth drew in a sharp breath, wondering if the attorney knew about Sue and Baby Ruthie.

"As I said yesterday, I don't play moral judge, and I believe that every person is entitled to fair representation in a court of law. Are you ready to put your trust in me?"

Beth decided to level with her. "You asked me yesterday if either Angie or I got off the ambulance to assist the patient. Angie was driving coked up to her eyeballs. At first, she thought we'd hit a pothole, so I got out to check. The girl was sprawled out in the street, hemorrhaging badly and about to give birth. I ran back to the ambulance for help, but Angie was so freaked out over hitting a pedestrian that she refused to help me or even radio in for back-up. Instead, she got back on the ambulance. I had to deliver the baby myself. The girl was hemorrhaging from her ears as well as her vagina, and there was no way I could assist her at the same time.

Jean was furiously taking notes on a pink legal pad. "What happened then?"

"I wrapped the baby in the bloody towel and put her into the ambulance, planning to drop her at the hospital. Angie was enraged that I had brought the baby on board and threatened to have me fired if I reported the accident. She said she'd tell the department I'd been the one driving. 'Who would they believe,' she said, 'a paramedic candidate who'd only been on the job for six weeks or a veteran who'd been with the department for fifteen years?'"

Beth paused, wondering if she dared go on with the truth. And then she remembered Sue's words, flung at her in anger: "Through your unscrupulous deeds, you've endangered the lives of eight children." And what of herself? She could be incarcerated for the rest of her life!

Looking the attorney straight in the eyes, she added: "Angie dropped me off at McDonalds and told me to keep my mouth shut. When she picked me up about twenty minutes later, the baby was gone. I don't know what she did with her. I was too scared to ask." Beth flinched at a sharp rap on the door.

"Ms. Edgar, is your client ready?"

Jean stood up, smiling brightly at Beth. "Well, if that's what happened, go ahead and tell them. Let's put an end to this mess, shall we?"

As Beth eased into a chair beside her attorney, she noted the presence of the female investigator who'd visited her house. Evidently she was going to be doing the questioning.

"Ms. Reilly, was your ambulance involved in a hit-and-run accident on Madison and Green on Monday morning, November 22, 1993?" asked Maggie O'Connor.

"That is correct."

"Who was driving the vehicle at the time of the accident?"

"My paramedic officer."

"Would that be Angela Ropella, now deceased?"

"She was my partner."

"How long had you been with the fire department before the accident?"

"About six weeks."

"What condition was your partner in before the accident?"

"She was high on coke."

"Did you know she'd banged the ambulance into a pedestrian?"

"Not at first. I thought we hit a pothole."

"So you got off the vehicle to check for damage?"

"Right."

Restlessly drumming her fingers on the table, Maggie leaned across the table. "When I was at your house, you told me that neither you nor Angie had exited the ambulance. Why the change in story?"

"I was confused. My captain had just died... I was getting over the flu."

"Let's just go on. What did you see when you got out?"

"I saw a young woman hemorrhaging in the last stage of labor."

"What was your partner doing?"

"She took one look at the woman and started screaming, 'Oh, my god, I'm going to lose my job.'"

"Did either of you radio in for assistance?"

"No." Beth squirmed.

"So you drove away from the accident scene without reporting it."

"Yes." Beth was beginning to feel like a two-year-old being reprimanded for wetting her pants.

"Beth, we've got a witness who says he saw you get off the back of the ambulance to attend to the patient."

Beth felt her stomach tightening.

"He says he saw you pick up what could have been a baby wrapped in a blanket and get back on the ambulance before you guys drove off."

"That's what I did. I wanted to get the baby to the hospital."

"Then why didn't you call it in?"

"Angie was hysterical. She threatened to have me fired if I reported the accident. She said she'd take care of this thing herself."

Maggie lowered her voice. "Where's the baby, Beth?

Beth started to weep. "I don't know. Angie dropped me at McDonald's, told me to keep my mouth shut, and she'd be back to pick me up."

"Why didn't you tell anyone?"

"I was scared. The woman was a cocaine freak. Who knows what she'd do to me?"

Maggie looked exasperated. "If you were that scared, why didn't you report her, have her arrested?"

Jean grabbed Beth's elbow, propelling her to a standing position. "Look, my client is cooperating. She's told you the whole story. What more do you want? I think it's time for this conversation to end."

"Fine." Maggie pulled out a pair of cuffs. "Beth Reilly, you're under arrest for failing to report a personal injury accident, leaving the scene of a personal injury accident, and kidnapping, and will be held at Cook County Jail pending a bond hearing."

Glancing at her attorney as she was being taken from the room, Beth couldn't believe this was actually happening. Thank God her parents weren't alive to see this.

Then the internal affairs director was in her face. "Beth

Reilly, you are hereby suspended from duty for aggravated kidnapping and committing a criminal offense while on duty. We will be launching our own investigation into this matter. If our findings concur with those of the police, your medical license will be revoked. Goodbye, Ms. Reilly."

A uniformed officer led Beth down the hall, Jean Edgar grimly bringing up the rear.

Outside her bungalow raindrops of a receding April shower still hung, like melted icicles, on budding leaves. The big kids were playing hopscotch in the driveway.

"Jessie, you let the little guys play, too, you hear?" Sue called out the window. Wringing out a cloth laden with flax soap and water, Sue bent down on her hands and knees to scrub the marred hardwood floor. Although the living room was supposedly off-limits to her younger foster children, they enjoyed zooming their tricycles back and forth across the furniture-free room during the long winter.

Tucking a long strand of blonde hair back into a loose bun, the foster mother leaned into her work. The sound of whimpering echoed through the baby monitor. Sue tossed the rag into the pail of dirty water. She was already halfway up the stairs when the doorbell summoned her back down to the foyer.

Sue swung the door open wide. "Jessie! You know you're supposed to bring the children in through the garage."

But it wasn't the kids. A tall, black woman holding a clipboard stood on the front-steps. "Sue Dotson?"

"Yes," she answered. "What can I do for you?"

The woman consulted the clipboard. "Your file indicates

we haven't gotten back to you since a year ago February. Sorry for any inconvenience."

Sue tensed. "And you are—?"

A flashed badge. "DCFS."

Chapter Twenty One

For two weeks, the media had been having a field day with the missing baby case. Eric Saunder's homecoming, following a fourteen-day university-sponsored art history tour to Rome, had been marred by newspaper headlines: Trial For Female Paramedic Accused of Kidnapping Baby.

The art professor scanned the news article, his eyes finally focusing on the last three paragraphs:

Fire department records indicate that,
in her five months as a paramedic candidate,
Reilly received Mayor Daley's firefighter's award
for saving the lives of an alderman and a former
police chief who had been food poisoned.
Firefighter Quinn Reynolds, Reilly's partner, says
Reilly once performed CPR on their firehouse
captain who had gone into cardiac arrest while
on duty.

"Reilly has no past criminal record."

Fishing a pocketknife from his back jeans pocket, Eric razed the two-column article from the Tribune. Beth had painted the scenario during their date at the veggie-diner: How her paramedic officer, high on coke, had banged into a pregnant homeless woman, delivered and then kidnapped the baby, leaving the young mother to hemorrhage to death in the streets. How the police would attempt to lay blame on her because she'd only been a paramedic for six weeks as opposed to her partner, a former Vietnam nurse, who'd been with the fire department for fifteen years.

Eric looked off into the distance, stroking his chin. "What to do, what to do." He and Beth had only gone out a few times, and the police did seem to have pretty solid evidence to pull her in.

Suddenly he shouted in glee. "A protest march against her wrongful incarceration!" Former teaching colleagues of her parents, medical library co-workers, and his own art history students would create quite a stir for the cameras.

Shoving his duffel bags aside, Eric snatched a sheet of paper from his oak desk, pulled out the university directory, and started compiling a list.

Jean Edgar watched the judge scan the courtroom as he listened to a police officer's testimony. Appointed to the bench during the "Days of Rage," Judge Robert Dolan's philosophy had swung from reform-minded to hard-core conservative within the last twenty-five years, leaving him a crusty intellectual with little patience for theatrics. Jean knew him to be a fair judge, but still worried as assistant states attorney, Jim Lamperi, questioned his first witness.

"Officer Hurowitz, where were you at approximately six a.m. on Monday, November twenty-second of last year?"

"Me and my partner were heading down Madison towards Zorba's for breakfast when we saw this woman lying in the street. Looked like she'd been hit by a car."

"Objection, your honor," Jean said. The witness is giving an opinion."

"Sustained. The court reminds the witness to stick to the facts."

"What was her condition?" continued the prosecuting attorney.

"Well, she wasn't breathing, and she was bleeding heavily. Her leg was mangled, and her head looked like a pancake."

"Objection."

"Overruled. The witness is describing what he saw."

"What did you do then?"

"We radioed for paramedics and the medical examiner."

"Did you notice where the bleeding was coming from, Officer Hurowitz?"

"Yeah, it was coming from the girl's ears and vagina."

"Thank you officer. No further questions."

Judge Dolan glanced questioningly at Jean, but she had no interest in cross-examining the officer. "You may call your next witness, Mr. Lamperi."

The prosecuting attorney got to his feet unhurriedly and approached the medical examiner. "How long have you been with the Cook County Coroner's Office, Dr. Sarietta?"

"Twenty-two years next month."

"Did you examine a young white female whom you later learned was Violet Williams?"

"Yes."

"What was the cause of death?"

"Upon examining unidentified white female ME #93-602, believed to be approximately eighteen years of age, I found a crushed skull, badly bruised face, broken femur, and evidence of internal hemorrhaging in the abdominal cavity."

"Dr. Sarietta, can you please describe your observations of the body?"

The medical examiner nodded. "There were a few stray white paint chips and shiny metal pieces on the hip area of the girl's dress—also tire-tracks on the clothing—indicating that a vehicle struck her and ran her over."

"Did you find any evidence linking this young woman with a recent pregnancy?"

"Objection. State is leading the witness."

"Sustained."

"Dr. Sarietta, did you observe anything else about the body?"

"When I opened her up, the girl had a ruptured uterus, as if she had just given birth a few hours before, but it was actually quite puzzling: the placenta was still intact, yet there was no sign of a baby."

"In your medical judgment, do you believe the victim gave birth spontaneously or was assisted?"

"From the clean cut of the umbilical cord, it would appear that a knowledgeable person was in attendance at time of birth."

"Possibly a paramedic?"

"Objection. Calls for speculation."

"Sustained."

"Thank you, Dr. Sarietta, that will be all."

"Martina Ramirez." Listening to the assistant state's attorney question his next witness, Jean quickly scanned the prosecution's witness list—no reference to 'Ramirez.' Par for the course.

"What is your job title?"

"I'm an emergency technician at Illinois Masonic Hospital."

Jean was on her feet. "Your honor, defense requests permission to approach the bench." Judge Dolan nodded, motioning for Jim to come forward also.

Jean whispered furiously. "Defense sees no mention of this witness on state's list."

The judge leaned forward, frowning. "What's up your sleeve today, Mr. Lamperi?"

The prosecuting attorney replied, his tone as smooth as cut glass. "The state had no idea this woman existed until seven a.m. this morning when she showed up at the police station, asking to testify."

The judge inclined his head towards Jean. "The volleyball's in your court, Ms. Edgar. What do you want to do?"

"Just go ahead with it, but first give me five minutes to confer with my client."

"Fine. Next time, Mr. Lamperi, do us all a favor and make like AT&T. Keep those lines of communication open."

"Yes, your honor," Jim said good-naturedly.

Jean returned to her seat. "Beth, do you know this woman?"

"She was on duty when I went back to the hospital for baby supplies."

"I don't recall you mentioning that you actually returned to the hospital after the accident."

"I must have forgotten."

"Listen, I'm not accepting any more surprises where you're concerned, do I make myself clear?" Jean whispered furiously.

"Sorry."

"Now what exactly, and I mean exactly, is the story behind the baby supplies?"

"I wanted to drop the baby off at the hospital. Angie said we'd go back to emergency, but only to pick up some baby supplies. When I got there, this new tech was hanging around, so I sent her on a phony expedition for medical supplies from the backroom. Meanwhile, I searched the cabinet in the hall. I found some diapers and Pedialyte, so I stuffed some bottles into my pockets and got out of there fast."

"Any more surprises and you're on your own."

Jim continued leading his witness through her testimony. "How long have you been on the job, Ms. Ramirez?"

"I transferred into emergency last November."

"Where were you at approximately five-thirty a.m. on Monday, November twenty-second of last year?

"Just finishing my shift at the hospital."

"Do you remember seeing a paramedic enter the premises around that time?"

"Yes."

"Do you see that person here today?"

The technician pointed at Beth. "That's her."

The attorney smiled. "Thank you. No further questions."

Jean stepped out from behind the desk she shared with Beth.

"Is it unusual to see a paramedic in emergency?"

"No, they're in and out of there all the time, bringing in patients or getting ambulance supplies."

"Then how can you be so sure it was my client you saw on hospital premises at that particular time?"

"She and her partner had just brought in a motorcycle-crash victim who'd been tossed across Lake Shore Drive. It's hard to forget something like that."

"So you saw my client with her partner."

"Yeah, but she came back about an hour later by herself. Asked for some backboards and splints."

"Was there anything unusual about that request?"

"Not really."

"No further questions."

Judge Dolan turned to the prosecution. "Does state wish to re-direct?"

Jim was already coming forward. "Yes, your honor. Ms. Ramirez, in your experience, do paramedics usually come back for supplies after already leaving the hospital?"

"Only when they're bringing in another patient."

"Yet you said the defendant came back alone."

"She said she'd forgotten a couple of items."

"Where are the emergency medical supplies kept?"

"The smaller supplies are organized in a cabinet in the hall, and the bigger stuff's kept in the backroom."

"So the backboards and splints were in the backroom?"

"Right."

"Did the defendant go back there with you?"

"No, she said she'd wait by the cabinet."

"Was she still there when you returned with her supplies?"

"I saw her take off just as I was coming down the hall."

"What did you do then?"

"Since I'd replenished the smaller supplies just before she got there, I decided to check out the cabinet."

"Did you notice anything missing?"

"A six-pack of two-inch nippled baby bottles filled with Pedialyte™ and some diapers."

"No further questions."

"Perfect," Jean mumbled under her breath.

"Does defense care to re-cross examine?"

"No, your honor."

Chapter Twenty Two

Jim Lamperi surreptitiously checked the john before spritzing his spiked hair one last time. At thirty-two, he was one of the youngest, most successful, first-chairs in the criminal court building. The door swung open and Ned Marcus, one of the junior partners, walked in. "Nice touch with the Ramirez witness."

Jim took a deep bow. "Thanks. It looks like Ms. Edgar's client failed to sprinkle some necessary twinkle-dust information in the attorney-client goody bag."

"Doesn't it faze you that the paramedic's getting so much media attention, as well as grassroots support from the academic community?" asked the junior partner.

"Listen, no matter what their IQ, the average person refuses to acknowledge the possibility that a middle-aged medical librarian turned paramedic could kidnap a newborn, leaving its mother to hemorrhage to death in the streets. That hits too close to home, Ned. They'd rather believe that Reilly's partner, a veteran paramedic officer and former Vietnam nurse hooked on drugs, disposed of the baby for fear of losing her job.

"And how about the defense's blank witness sheet?" grinned Ned.

"You mean the Witnesses for the Defense with a big red *0* scrawled on it?" said Jim, in mock surprise. "That had me thrown for a loop for a total of two seconds until I figured it out: Edgar's going for the tear-jerker, where the accused, cowed by her excursion into the inferno, impales herself on the mercy of the court.

"No way is Little Miss Pure-As-The-Driven-Snow getting off the hook, Ned. By the time I empty my bag of tricks, she'll be in the slammer for the next millennium."

"Good luck, man," said the junior partner, walking out the door.

The prosecuting attorney stared at himself in the bathroom mirror, jerking on his tie one last time. "And I'll be on my way to an associate judgeship, he whispered."

Huddled in the witness chair, RJ's sullen posture symbolized his reluctance to testify. But Jim was an old hand with wary witnesses.

"Firefighter Sloan, how long have you been with the Chicago Fire Department?"

"Seven years."

"Were you on duty Monday, November twenty-second at six-thirty a.m.?"

"Yep. My shift wasn't over until eight a.m."

"Did you have occasion to observe Ambulance Sixty at the end of the shift?"

"Be kind of hard to miss. We only got one ambulance at the firehouse."

"Did you notice anything about the grille on the vehicle?"

"Yeah, it was dented."

"By the way, who was your commanding officer?"

"Captain Julian Paine."

"Anything unusual about your captain's relationship with the defendant?"

"Yeah. He didn't like her."

"No further questions."

Jean clasped the podium as she cross-examined the witness. "Did you observe Ambulance Sixty at the beginning of the shift?"

"No. We were out on a run."

"Then you don't know if that damage was already there?"

"Uh-uh."

"Isn't it true that most of the vehicles in your garage are constantly getting dented up?"

"Yeah, it happens. We don't make a big deal about a dent."

Jean passed him an ID photo. "Do you know this person?"

RJ gingerly took the photo. "Yeah, that's Angie Ropella. She was the driver on 'Sixty'."

"No further questions."

Climbing the courtroom stairs flanked by television news cameras and flashing lights, her arm held by her attorney, Beth no longer feared being among a sea of hardened criminals. So comfortable was she among the vast array of court reporters, attorneys, and judges that she had to constantly remind herself that she was on "the other side"—an accused felon.

Yes, adversity was turning her into a great pretender. Not long ago she'd scorned Sue for that same moral transformation from criminal accomplice to Madonna. It was easy to fake one's innocence with a plausible tale, especially with the media and grassroots supporters rooting for you.

She didn't know how Eric Saunders had pulled it off, but ever since the trial began, the art history professor had somehow managed to have at least half-a-dozen protesters from the U. of C. in daily attendance outside the courtroom building, carrying signs and shouting slogans: "Free Beth, free Beth!"

She had Sue to thank for introducing her to Eric, just as she had her to thank for convincing Reverend Luke to secure an attorney in her behalf. And though she'd never admit it to Jean, she felt lucky to have found protection under the older woman's forthright, empathetic wing. Deep down, she acknowledged that Jean probably bestowed that protective shield upon all her clients, wealthy or indigent, guilty or innocent.

Beth knew Jean didn't buy her story about Angie kidnapping the baby. She ached to tell her the truth, but her life, as well as the lives of Sue, her seven foster kids and Baby Ruthie, were at stake. She'd heard that the homeless victim had been identified; perhaps a family member would come forward to claim the baby if her whereabouts were made public.

Then again, maybe not. The young woman had been homeless. Perhaps parental abuse or neglect forced her into the streets. The baby was bi-racial. If a family member failed to identify her, she could be stuck in limbo at DCFS for years. Undoubtedly,

Beth was doing the right thing, protecting all of them through her silence.

A palpable tension commanded the crowded courtroom.

"Someone must have leaked that the state's sole eye-witness will testify today," Jean muttered to Beth.

Prosecuting attorney Jim Lamperi commenced his questioning.

"Traffic specialist O'Connor, how long have you been with the Chicago Police Department?"

"Five years."

"Were you involved in the investigation of the vehicular homicide of Violet Williams?"

"Yes."

"Please explain what actions you initially took in the investigation."

"After finding out from the medical examiner that the girl had given birth but there was no baby present, my partner and I checked all the medical clinics, hospitals, churches, and garbage dumpsters in the vicinity. We found no sign of an abandoned newborn."

"What did you do then?"

"We showed the girl's picture to the homeless shelter coordinator and residents of The Olive Mission. An older guest remembered seeing a young, white pregnant woman going by the name of 'Violet'. Said the girl was in there the night before the accident, asking around for free clinics and adoption agencies."

"What action did you take after receiving this information?"

"Since we had no ID on the girl, we faxed her morgue photo to police agencies all over the state."

"Did you receive any leads based upon that photo?"

"Not until recently."

"What did you find out?"

"The girl's name was Violet Williams; she was eighteen years old and resided in Chilicothe, Illinois."

"Traffic specialist O'Connor, did you have occasion to interview Paramedic Reilly concerning her participation in the hit-and-run accident of November twenty-second?"

"On two separate occasions."

"Did the defendant's responses prove similar?"

"Objection!" cried Jean. "Counsel is leading the witness."

"Sustained," said Judge Dolan. "The witness may answer the question."

"Paramedic Reilly initially stated that neither she nor her partner exited the ambulance before leaving the accident scene. She later retracted her story, claiming that both she and her partner left the vehicle to examine the victim."

"Thank you, Specialist O'Connor. You may step down."

Lamperi now summoned to the stand the mother of the victim.

"Please state your name."

"Mary Jean Williams."

"And where do you reside?"

"Chilicothe, Illinois."

Jim handed her a picture. "Who's that?"

"That's my girl."

"When's the last time you saw her?"

"Last June. She was staying with her aunt in Peoria since graduation."

His voice softened as he handed her the faxed photo. "Ever seen this before?"

Her face paled and she fell back in her seat.

"Mrs. Williams, are you all right?" Jim asked solicitously.

"I'm sorry. It's still such a shock seeing her that way."

"So you have seen this photo before?"

She nodded. "Deputy Aarons showed it to my husband and me last November."

"Is this your daughter?"

"Yes."

"No further questions."

Deputy Sam Aaron clicked the last suitcase lock into place as he listened to the brief testimony of Mary Jean William's on Court TV. The detective from the CPD had assured him she would only testify as a life-death witness, and that's how it had panned out. It took a lot of guts for a woman, abused for years, to come forward and identify the morgue photo of her only daughter despite her husband's threats.

"If only he'd cared more for his daughter than his reputation," she'd wept, "Violet could have come back and had the baby—and she'd still be alive today.

Shortly after the Chicago Police Department had come snooping into the Williams' cover-up, the sheriff had given Sam his walking papers. But he had no regrets. Justice had been served.

Addie had backed his decision to rent out their house and renew their relationship with Grandpa Aaron in Chicago. Sam was setting his sights on joining the CPD. Hopefully, it would be a great place to raise their son.

Locking the door to his little house for the last time, the words of Mary Jean Williams ran fitfully through his brain. "What's to become of me now, Sam? Once I testify, I'll be about as welcome in Chilicothe as a torn heifer."

Sam prayed that Mary Jean Williams, now an outcast in the town of her ancestors, would find the strength to start over again.

Chapter Twenty Three

"The state calls Jerry Jablowski to the stand."

A short, reedy man with bloodshot eyes shuffled toward the stand.

"Do you swear to tell the truth, the whole truth, so help you God?

"Yeah."

"You may sit down."

"Mr. Jablowski, please state your occupation for the court."

"Night janitor for Teletrac."

"How long have you been working there?"

"Since last September."

"Please tell the court what you saw on Monday, November twenty-second at six a.m."

"I open the side door to shake out my dust mop and I seen an accident."

"What kind of accident?"

"This ambulance banged into a girl crossing the street."

"Was there a number on the ambulance?"

"Yeah. Number sixty.'"

"The accident happened nearly six months ago, Mr. Jablowski. How can you be so sure that's the number you saw?"

"Cause it was my old man's sixtieth birthday."

"Did you see anybody get off the ambulance to check on the victim?"

"Objection," Jean called out. "The state is leading the witness."

"Overruled," said Judge Dolan.

"Yeah, some lady in a blue uniform."

"Which door did she used to exit the vehicle?"

"She got out through the double doors in back."

"Then what happened?"

"She kneels down by this girl for a couple minutes. Then she runs back to the ambulance."

"Then what happened?"

"Then another lady and her run back to check out the girl."

"Was the second woman also wearing a blue uniform?"

"Yeah."

"Did both paramedics stay with the victim?"

"Uh-uh. The first lady grabs the second lady, but the second one pushes her away. Then the second lady runs back to the ambulance and slams the door."

"Which door did the second paramedic use to get back on the ambulance?"

"The passenger's side."

"What happened then?"

"The first lady kneels down by this girl in the street for a long time."

"And then?"

"She gets up, holding something in her arms. It looked like a baby in a blanket."

"A baby?"

"Yeah, she was kind of cradling it in her arms."

"Then what happened, Mr. Jablonski?"

"Then she takes off in the ambulance."

"Did the police have you identify that paramedic in a photo line-up?"

"Uh-huh."

"Mr. Jablowski, is the paramedic who took that baby sitting here today?"

Jablowski stared at Beth through indifferent eyes. "Yeah, that's her."

"No further questions."

Tearing off her horn rimmed glasses, Jean leaped to her feet, her voice ringing through the courtroom. "Mr. Jablowski, isn't it true that you have been arrested twice on burglary charges and are currently incarcerated for breaking and entering the company you work for?"

"That's right."

"Isn't it also true that you've worked out some kind of plea bargain with the state if you testify against my client?"

"Hey, lady, I saw what I saw."

"What was the weather like the morning of the accident, Mr. Jablowski?"

"It was real foggy."

"About how far away from the accident were you standing?"

"Maybe a block down."

"From that distance, how could you be certain that a baby was wrapped in that blanket?"

"The paramedic was rocking it back and forth."

"It could have been a dog, or even a doll."

"Naw, the medic was kneeling in the street right before it happened."

"Despite this thick fog and being four-hundred feet away from the accident, you're sure its my client you saw running back to the ambulance holding a baby."

"Sure."

"Were you working alone that morning?"

"Yup."

"Had anything to drink?"

"Nope."

"Any parked cars between you and her?"

"Uh-uh."

"You initially identified my client from a photo line-up."

"Yeah."

"I'd like you to shut your eyes and describe my client."

"Okay. She got curly reddish brown hair cut kind of short, greenish eyes, 'bout five-foot-five and she ain't had a pepperoni and cheese for a long time." He chortled, scratching at his side like a flea-bitten dog.

Jean calmly handed the witness an ID photo. "Is this the photo you used to identify my client?"

A brief look of uncertainty. crossed his face. "I think so."

"Yes or no?"

He held the picture eye-level, then squinted at Beth from across the room.

"Do you wear glasses?"

"Naw, I just wanted to make sure."

"Is this or is this not, a picture of the paramedic you saw running back to the ambulance clutching a baby in her arms?"

"Well, her hair looks a little darker in the picture but she could have dyed it."

"Just answer the question."

"Yeah, that's her."

Confidently handing the photo to the judge, Jean picked another from her pocket and laid it before the witness. "Do you see anybody in this room resembling this photo ID?"

"What kind of crap is this? I answered all your questions and now you're trying to trick me."

"Watch your language, sir, you're in a court of law. Are you saying this is the paramedic you saw running from the ambulance?"

"I just said so, didn't I?"

Handing the second picture to the judge, Jean said, "Let the records show the witness identified both ID pictures as my client. In fact, ID number one is a photo of Angie Ropella, my client's deceased paramedic officer, who slammed her ambulance—"

Lamperi was on his feet. "Objection!"

Judge Dolan banged his gavel.

"—into the hit-and-run victim—"

"Objection!"

"—then left the scene of the crime, leaving a young pregnant girl who had just given birth to hemorrhage to death in the street."

The prosecuting attorney hammered his fist on the desk before him. "Objection, Your Honor. Defense is slandering a person unable to defend herself from these brutal accusations."

The judge growled at Jean. "Counsel, when objection is made, you will stop and await my ruling."

"I'm sorry your honor," Jean smiled back apologetically.

Jim's eyes were two slits, his face pale in rage. "I ask that counsel's entire statement be stricken from the record."

The judge held up his hand for silence. "It shall be stricken. Does the state have any further witnesses to call?"

"No, Your Honor."

"This court is adjourned until 10:00 am Thursday."

Jim drummed his fingers on the sushi bar as he waited for his luncheon companion. She was already a half-hour late and he'd had enough saki to sink a sub. Right now, he could be holed up with the new blonde he'd met at Ditka's last week. Instead, he was courting some uptight social worker who could update him on what was going on inside the juvenile system. He needed as much information as possible when he was appointed a juvenile judge.

It hadn't happened yet, but this kidnapping case was going to push him over the edge.

He'd been slightly jarred the day before when Jean Edgar had verbally pummeled his star witness, but he hadn't been surprised. "No matter how you dress and coach a shmuck like Jablowski, nobody's going to believe a three-time petty thief beyond the shadow of a doubt, even when he's on the level," he murmured.

Lamperi needed hard evidence to send Beth Reilly cascading down the waterfall. Gulping down the last of his saki, Jim grabbed his briefcase and was just heading for the door when a tall, fashionably dressed black woman hurried toward him.

"Sorry I'm late, but I was interviewing this foster mom who had no ID on a six-month-old, bi-racial baby in her care. Bizarre!"

Jim's antennae went up. The baby kidnapped by Beth Reilly fit that description. Could it be more than coincidence?

Smiling, he steered her toward the bar. "Who says DCFS is all fucked up?" he whispered in her ear.

Chapter Twenty Four

"Y ou got a visitor," the guard said, shoving the key into the cell door.

"You're kidding," said Beth. "No one's been to visit me in the last two weeks except for my attorney."

"Well there's a guy out there asking to see you now. You wanna see him or not?"

Beth glanced down at her blue prison uniform. "I'm not exactly dressed for visitors."

"Want me to tell him to leave?"

"No, no, I'll see him."

"Then let's move it. I got another prisoner to check in."

As the guard led her down the hall, Beth silently ticked off the names of possible visitors. Maybe her partner Quinn. Possibly Wally or Don from the firehouse. She'd played basketball with them a few times between runs. But she'd only been with the department for six months; they didn't owe her any loyalty.

A former colleague from U. of C.? Unlikely. As a medical librarian, she had preferred books over peers. In fact, only one of her former colleagues had contacted her since her parents' funeral last year, and that was to retrieve a reference book she'd borrowed.

Since her visitor was male, it obviously couldn't be Sue, although she was yearning to see both her and Ruthie. Reverend Luke threatened to take Sue's kids if she attempted to resume their friendship. How many times had she told her best friend not to trust that slime ball?

She and Sue had their fill of arguments over the years, Beth thought, as the guard steered her toward the visitation room. Since high school, Sue had castigated her for always acting impulsively, especially when her taste in men switched from intellectuals to truck drivers.

"Honey, you go through men faster than a shopping mall," Sue would complain. "You've got to take other people's feelings into consideration."

"At least I don't let other people live my life for me," she'd retort.

But after a few days of giving each other the silent treatment, they always made up. The silence had never lasted this long. Still, she could see how asking your best friend to aid and abet in a kidnapping could stretch a friendship past its breaking point!

Guards flanked the back of the visitation room as Beth entered in handcuffs. Taking a seat behind the thick plaited glass, she saw Eric, wearing a crew-neck T-shirt underneath a black gabardine suit, walk toward her.

"Eric, what a surprise," she said, smiling warmly.

"I thought you could use a friend," he said, straightening his jacket as he sat down opposite her.

"Could I ever! Nobody loves a kidnapper," she said wryly.

"Alleged kidnapper. They haven't proved anything yet, right?"

"Whether they prove it or not, my career as Wonder Woman is kaput."

"Maybe you could get back in at the library, at least temporarily. Your replacement took a maternity leave."

"After disgracing the names of my parents as well as myself? The University might just as well hire a garbage collector. But let's not talk about that. How did your art lecture tour go?"

"My students were enraptured with Paris."

Beth leaned forward, her face almost touching the glass. "Listen, I really appreciate the little charade you've been throwing in my honor."

"Excuse me?"

"Protesters marching in front of the court house every morning, holding up 'Free Beth' posters."

"You have more friends at the University than you think. Anyway, after those dead fetus posters, it was definitely time for some new art work."

"I especially like the rainbows. They make me feel like maybe I'll actually get out of this place before I grow senile."

"Don't talk crazy. Of course you'll get out. You're innocent, aren't you?" He smiled reassuringly.

Beth sighed. "Innocence is like truth—all in the eyes of the beholder."

Eric slid his chair closer to the plated glass. "What are you talking about?"

She felt a tap on her shoulder. "Visiting time is over," said the guard, pulling her to her feet.

"Check it out with Sue," she shouted over her shoulder.

Eric watched quizzically as Beth disappeared behind the closed door. Then he rushed out of the visitation room.

"I don't understand why you're not calling any witnesses on my behalf," Beth said between clenched teeth as Jean forcefully guided her past the flashing lights and intrusive reporters.

"We've been through this a dozen times, Beth. You lack an eyewitness to validate your story, and character witnesses are useless in this situation."

"What do you mean 'useless'? My life's on the line, isn't it? Why can't you put some people on the stand who worked with me at the university or the firehouse?"

"There are only certain things a character witness can vouch for. In your case, none of it applies."

"How 'bout how I saved the life of my fire captain after he went into cardiac arrest at the firehouse?"

"All of this would be useful for sentencing following a guilty verdict. Let's hope it doesn't come to that."

"Fine. Underneath that pretense of empathy, you're sending me down the river in a holey raft."

"Don't be absurd."

"The only person who can help me now is me. I want you to put me on the stand."

"I might as well toss a newborn into a lion pit."

Beth blanched at visions of Baby Ruthie as the tossee.

"I don't care what you say. I'm going into that court room and tell my story."

Jean paused. "And what story might that be?"

"You told me it didn't matter!" Beth spat.

"I told you I'd represent you, innocent or guilty, because each person is entitled to due process of the law. But I sense that you're still holding back."

Beth whispered. "You know all you need to know."

"You realize the prosecution will attempt to decimate your story."

"I can handle it."

"They'll try to confuse you."

"I don't confuse easily."

"One false move could land you in jail."

"Look, I'm fighting for my existence, and I'm going to do whatever it takes to protect myself and—"

"And who, Beth?"

"Never mind."

"Well, I guess that's decided then," said Jean, standing to signal an end to their meeting.

"By the way," Jean said, nonchalantly bending for her briefcase, "Is it true that your parents were involved in some kind of genetic testing before you were born?"

Beth gawked at her. "How did you know?"

"You continue to underestimate me! I've defended clients with secrets much more sinister than yours. Now: What about the testing?"

"When my parents were graduate students at the University of Chicago, they earned some extra pocket money by participating in a genetic testing experiment. At the time, they were told the drug they were given was perfectly safe, but later, they learned that their offspring would be sterile."

"How old were you when they shared this information?"

"Thirty-eight. They were killed in a car collision shortly after telling me."

Jean looked at her incredulously. "So that's why you took the baby."

"What?"

"The emotional trauma of being told you were sterile, coupled with guilt over your parents death, threw you over the edge."

"Since when are you a psychologist?" Beth taunted.

"By bringing that baby into the world, you were resurrecting your parents," Jean murmured.

"I've been away from church too long to be talking resurrection."

"We could plead temporary insanity."

"Forget it. I'm going for broke."

"Aren't you the least bit frightened?"

Beth smiled and shook her head. "I've got too much at stake to be scared."

The courtroom artist sketched a woman of medium height, dressed in a navy blue skirt suit and high-necked white blouse as she purposefully walked toward the stand. Self-assured and confident, noted a Chicago Tribune reporter.

"Beth, how long have you been a paramedic with the Chicago Fire Department?" Jean asked pleasantly.

"I've been a paramedic candidate for almost six months."

"What was your previous occupation?"

"I was a medical librarian at the University of Chicago."

"For how long?"

"Fifteen years."

"What made you decide to change careers mid-stream?"

"My parents were killed in a multi-car collision last year. After hearing how two paramedics tried to save them, I decided to follow in their footsteps."

"In the six months you've been with the department, have you received any special recognition for your heroics?"

Beth nodded. "I received a medal from the mayor for saving an alderman and former police chief from food poisoning, and I saved my captain's life when he went into cardiac arrest at the firehouse."

"You mentioned earlier that you are a paramedic candidate. Can you explain to the court the difference between a candidate and a full-fledged paramedic?"

"I became a paramedic candidate after taking a three month academic and physical endurance training program at the Fire Academy. After graduating, I signed on with the Chicago Fire Department and then was assigned to work with a paramedic officer for one year."

"Someone who presumably knows the ropes."

"Right."

"And your paramedic officer was Angela Ropella, now deceased?"

"That's correct."

"To your knowledge, Beth, how long had your PO been a paramedic?"

"Seventeen years. Prior to that, she was a nurse in Vietnam."

"What was it like working with someone of that caliber?"

"I only trained with her for six weeks, but I found her to be dedicated, and resourceful."

"Resourceful?"

"She always knew what to do, no matter what the situation. I was absolutely in awe of her. And she was fearless, too."

"How so?"

"Once we got a call for a gunshot wound at Cabrini Green. She'd forgotten her bulletproof vest, but that didn't stop her. She told me to wait in the ambulance and went in there herself. It was a ninth floor unit and the elevators were out. Ten minutes later, she was out of there, the victim on a stretch cot."

"Did you have any reason to suspect that Angie was doing coke?"

"I wasn't a medical librarian for nothing."

"What did you do?"

"I dropped some hints around the firehouse, but nobody was particularly concerned. Evidently, Angie had been doing drugs since Vietnam when her fiancé, an army doctor, was killed by a grenade. The guys told me nobody had ever reported her. Somehow, her drug problem never seemed to interfere with her job performance, if anything, it made her more of a risk taker."

"Did you report her drug habit to your superiors?"

"After just making a mid-life career change? No way. A paramedic candidate lacks union representation. In a best-case scenario, Angie would go into a 'last chance' substance abuse program, but I'd be kicked off the department as a snitch."

"So you were just biding your time until your candidacy year was up?"

"An intelligent person learns to adapt. Besides, I was learning textbooks just watching Angie deal with the patients."

"Did you notice anything unusual about Angie's behavior on the morning of the accident?"

"Just that she seemed more hyper than usual."

"How so?"

"We'd just dropped this boy at Masonic who had been mangled in a motorcycle crash. He'd lost a lot of blood and didn't look like he was going to make it, but Angie managed to keep him going until we got to the hospital. The kid couldn't have been more than sixteen Angie seemed really shaken. After we dropped the patient in emergency, she headed for the bathroom. Back on the ambulance, she was Ms. Bright Eyes again."

"What were you doing at the time of the accident?"

"I was in the back straightening up supplies when I felt a jolt."

"What happened then?"

"I jumped off the rig to check out the damage."

"Where was Angie?"

"She'd been knocked against the steering wheel and was looking kind of dazed."

"What happened after you exited the ambulance?"

"I found a young Caucasian woman lying in a pool of blood about fifty feet from the rig. Upon examining her, I found a broken femur, a crushed skull, and blood seeping from the ears. She was also in transition."

"Transition?"

"About to give birth. The head was already crowning."

"Was Angie still on the ambulance at this time?"

"No, she exited the ambulance, swearing because she thought she'd hit a pothole. It was foggy that morning, so at first she didn't see the girl. When she saw that we hit a pedestrian, she became hysterical, screaming that she'd be fired if the department found out she'd been driving high."

"What happened then?"

"She was acting so nuts, I panicked. There was no way I

could attend to a dying woman plus deliver the baby at the same time. But then Angie kneeled down to examine the girl. When she saw the head crowning, she shouted for me to go back to the ambulance for supplies. When I offered to assist, she pushed me away."

"You'd only been a paramedic for six weeks at the time of the accident. Had you ever delivered a baby prior to that time?"

"No."

"Being with the Department for such a brief span of time, were you allowed to attend to a patient on your own?"

"Yes."

"What happened then?"

"Once I got back to the ambulance, I grabbed some supplies and attempted to radio for assistance, but Angie was already mounting the stairs holding the baby. When she saw what I was doing, she knocked my hand off the radio, screaming that she'd tell everybody I'd been the one driving the ambulance if I reported the accident."

"How did you react to Angie's threat?"

"I was frantic. 'What about the girl?' I asked. 'We can't just leave her to hemorrhage to death.' But Angie started the motor and told me to forget the whole thing ever happened.

"And what did you do?"

"I was screaming at her by this time, telling her we had to get the baby to the hospital. Angie laid the baby in between the armrests of the two front seats. "We'll stop back at Masonic," she said, "but only for baby supplies."

"So you returned to Masonic once again?"

"Right. I was searching the hallway cabinet for baby formula and diapers when the hospital tech saw me. I sent her on a fake expedition for backboard and splints, grabbed what I needed, and split."

"Then what happened?"

"When I got back on the ambulance, Angie was all cool and collected. What are we going to do with the baby?' I asked. 'She's no longer your concern,' she answered. By that time, she'd pulled up in front of McDonald's. She dropped me off there, told me not to even consider doing anything stupid then drove off. When she returned a half-hour later, the baby was gone.

"I asked her what she did with the baby, and she told me she was somewhere safe. As we pulled up to the firehouse, she said, 'Should you ever decide to clear your conscience, you should know that I've recorded my recollection of this morning's events. Of course, the details are slightly modified.'

"I was crying by this time, and Angie patted me on the back, saying that if I kept my mouth shut everything would be okay. She OD'd not long after. The guilt of what she'd done—"

"Objection," yelled Jim. "Conclusion by the defendant."

"Sustained," ruled the judge.

Like a skilled puppeteer, Jean allowed her client's last words to hang in the air before proceeding.

"Do you have any knowledge of the baby's whereabouts?"

"None at all."

"No further questions, your honor."

Judge Dolan banged his gavel. "The defendant may step down. Court is adjourned until nine a.m. tomorrow."

* * *

Back at the lock up, Jean congratulated Beth. "I must admit, you do render a convincing story."

, Beth breathed a sigh of relief.

Chapter Twenty Five

Attorney Jim Lamperi glanced quickly at the jury as they stood to allow Judge Dolan to enter the courtroom. While their faces were appropriately blank for the beginning of the day, yesterday's murmurings had been intense following Reilly's incriminating testimony against her partner. "Give the jurors a good line and they suck it up every time."

Media coverage inside the courtroom sure as hell didn't help. On the stand, Reilly came across sincere and self-assured. Hell, he would have swallowed her testimony, himself, had he not become acquainted with a few choice facts.

"Do you wish to cross-examine the witness, Mr. Lamperi?" asked the judge.

Jim stood up, straightening his tie. "Yes, your honor." Proceeding toward the witness box, he asked, "Ms. Reilly, you testified that your paramedic officer was driving Ambulance Sixty at the time of the accident. Is that correct?"

"Yes."

"And you both exited the vehicle."

"That's right."

"When she sent you back to the ambulance for supplies, which door did you use?"

"The passenger side."

"Was she holding the baby when she returned to the vehicle?"

"Yes."

"Which door did she use?"

Beth hesitated momentarily. "The driver's side."

"Yet, an eye-witness testified that he saw the second paramedic climb in through the passenger side."

Beth felt faint.

"Objection, your honor," screamed Jean. "This is all hearsay."

"Sustained," ruled Judge Dolan. "Mr. Lamperi is restating testimony already on record."

The state's attorney abruptly switched gears. "Ms. Reilly, approximately what time did your partner drop you off at McDonalds the morning of the accident?"

Beth blinked. "Approximately 6:15 a.m."

"And this was after you confiscated the baby supplies from the hospital?"

"Objection!" Jean called out.

"Sustained," ruled the judge. "Non-inflammatory words will be sufficient, Mr. Lamperi."

"Sorry, your honor." The state's attorney smiled boyishly. "Would it be accurate to say that you already had the baby supplies in your possession at the time?"

"Yes."

"And you had already delivered the baby."

"Angie delivered the baby."

"Of course. How would you describe the condition of your uniform?"

"Bloody."

"Paramedic Reilly, why was your uniform bloody if you neither delivered nor assisted in delivering the baby?"

The sound of her beating heart pounded in Beth's ears as she searched for a quick response. "I was attending to the infant's mother; she was hemorrhaging through the ears."

"While you were at the hospital, did you attempt to clean up?"

"At the time, personal hygiene wasn't my number one priority."

"And you made no stops between the hospital and McDonald's?"

"Correct."

"So your blues looked awfully grisly by the time your partner dropped you at McDonalds."

"That's right."

"Paramedic Reilly, doesn't 'awfully grisly' more aptly describe a uniform that's been splattered during childbirth rather than bloodied by hemorrhaging through the ears?"

Jean Edgar jumped up in disgust. "Objection, your honor. Prosecution is asking my client to speculate on various degrees of blood stains!"

"Sustained." Judge Dolan hit his gavel. "Switch tracks, Mr. Lamperi."

"Yes, your honor," Jim smiled ingratiatingly. "Paramedic Reilly, how often did you and your partner venture into McDonald's?" asked Lamperi, pacing back and forth, his head down, hands clasped behind his back.

"Just about every day."

"So you were regulars?"

"I guess you could call us that."

"How many cashiers usually work the front?"

"Maybe two, three. Different days, different shifts."

"You knew the cashiers by sight and vice versa."

"Right."

"They wear name tags, don't they?"

"I guess." Beth began to feel queasy.

"Was there some breakfast special you usually ordered?"

"Your honor, I don't see where this line of questioning is leading," said Jean.

"Sustained," ruled the judge. "Mr. Lamperi, if you have a point to make, make it."

"Did your food orders involve anything unusual?"

"Not really. I always order a scrambled egg and biscuit, with hot water and lemon."

"What's the name of the clerk who served you?"

Beth's face reddened. "I'm not sure. I don't think I ordered that morning anyway, I was too upset."

"Even so, a whole string of cashiers would have to be comatose to miss seeing one of their regulars in a uniform you agreed was 'grisly!'"

Beth was silent.

"In fact, you never entered McDonald's the morning of November twenty-second," Jim shouted.

Fear caught up with her. "That's a lie!"

"Objection, your honor." Jean was on her feet. "Counsel is browbeating the witness."

"Overruled," intoned the judge. "Mr. Lamperi's logic is sound."

Taking advantage of the defendant's shock at his barrage, Jim turned polite. "Paramedic Reilly, would you describe for the court your relationship with Julian Paine, now deceased?"

Beth paled. Jean had assured her that the judge would not permit questions concerning the captain's death.

"Are you all right?" asked the prosecuting attorney solicitously.

Beth willed herself to respond. "He was captain at the firehouse where I was assigned."

"Can you describe his conduct towards you?"

She took a deep breath. "Captain Paine was extremely demanding of his crew, especially the women."

"Demanding?"

"He expected the firehouse to be a Lysol monument."

"Isn't it true that he was so obsessive about cleanliness that he once threw a used sanitary pad at you across the crew table?" Jim asked innocently.

The jurors gasped as Beth winced. "He said women didn't belong in the firehouse."

"How many female crew members were assigned to your firehouse?"

"Two, Angie and myself. The captain thought that number was extreme."

"Would you say there was anything else that pointed to excess in his behavior towards you?"

Beth paused for an instant, remembering Jean's advice to steer clear of discussing her captain's sexual indulgences.

"Captain Paine kept a high profile in the crew locker room."

"Meaning?"

Her words came out as a sigh. "The guys at the firehouse were always joking about really giving the captain something to look at during one of his nocturnal locker searches."

"So you're saying your captain was a snoop."

"That's putting it mildly."

"Who cleaned out your partner's locker upon her death?"

"Captain Paine."

"Was this customary?"

"For him, yes."

The attorney leaned over and handed Beth a small book. "Does this look familiar?"

Beth glanced at the worn red cover. "It looks like my partner's work diary."

"Was it something she usually kept hidden away?"

"She used to keep it in her locker. She'd fill in entries every morning. In case she ever wanted to write a book, she said."

"Ms. Reilly, isn't it true that your captain confiscated Angie's diary implicating you as the kidnapper, and that he subsequently visited you at home and attempted to blackmail you into quitting the fire department?"

Beth sat rooted to her chair, too shocked to speak.

"Objection, your honor." Jean shouted from her table. "This is all conjecture."

"Sustained." Judge Dolan banged his gavel. "Mr. Lamperi, I will not have these unfounded speculations discussed as fact. Counsel's last comments will be stricken from the record."

Lamperi smiled smugly as he returned to his seat. "No further questions, your honor."

An audible whisper arose in the courtroom. Reporters were writing furiously. Judge Dolan banged his gavel. "Another outburst like this and we'll clear the court. Does defense wish to re-direct?"

"Yes, your honor." Jean was on her feet, moving like lightning to her client's side. "What time did you and Angie typically stop for breakfast?"

Still stinging from the prosecuting attorney's verbal attack, Beth answered meekly. "Somewhere between six-fifteen a.m. and six forty-five a.m., depending on our runs."

"How crowded is the restaurant at that time of morning?"

"There's always a handful of homeless people sitting in the back and several professional people being waited on up front."

"What door do you usually come in?"

"The front."

"And on the morning of November twenty-second?"

"I was distraught and looked like hell so I came in the side door entrance and just sat there until Angie came back."

"No further questions, your honor."

Judge Dolan banged his gavel. "Court is adjourned until nine a.m. tomorrow."

Chapter Twenty Six

Mary Jean Williams sat alone in a motel room at the Quality Inn, cradling the phone under her chin as she talked to the one safe link to her hometown.

"...and with four kids to raise, seven grandkids to tend, and the town grill to run. I ain't been up here to Chicago for 20 years. Lord knows, John Paul wouldn't never have let me come anyhow."

"Is John Paul that baby's father, Mary Jean?" Former Deputy Sam Aaron's voice echoed through the telephone.

"Truth's always been a grasshopper in my life. I'm just not sure, Sam. Matt had it bad for Violet, too."

"Somethin' fierce must have drove you to testify, braving John Paul's strong fist and the disdain of your three grown sons."

Mary Jean picked up the complimentary newspaper copy left outside her room that morning. As her eyes slowly captured each word of the first-page account of testimony involving the paramedic accused of kidnapping her daughter's baby, she shook her head in sorrow.

"I had to stand up for Violet, like I ain't never done when she was alive. I gotta go now, Sam." Swiping at her tears with the back of her hand, Mary Jean replaced the telephone receiver and tossed the newspaper aside.

"It just don't feel right a veteran paramedic would kidnap Violet's baby," she muttered, falling back on her paisley-print bedspread.

Jim confidently approached the jurors. "Ladies and gentlemen, truth is like a crystal; its clarity shines through from every angle. And it's crystal clear that, right from the get-go, Paramedic Candidate Beth Reilly made some deadly choices. First, the defendant kept her senior officer's drug problem under-wraps just so she could continue to reap the benefits of her expertise. Next, she neglected to report a hit-and-run accident, a call she could have made anonymously from a pay phone. Decency demands courage.

"The defense wants you to believe that Angie Ropella, hysterical over jeopardizing her career, got rid of the baby, all on her own. But planning and strategizing characteristics more aptly describe the exacting nature of a former medical librarian than that of a cocaine addict.

"Beth Reilly, childless and devoted to her career, lived alone with her parents for thirty-nine years. Faced with the opportunity of confiscating a dying woman's baby for her own, she took full advantage of the situation, later pushing the whole fiasco off on her dead partner. Adjusting his silver gray tie, the attorney momentarily turned to preen for the *Chicago Tribune* sketch artist, then returned to face the jury.

"How do we know for sure? Eyewitness Jerry Jablowski saw the accident from less than a block away. He positively identified the defendant as the paramedic who delivered Violet William's baby, wrapped the infant in a blanket, and hopped back on the ambulance without giving a backward glance toward the young mother hemorrhaging to death in the street. The medical examiner told you that the medical professional delivering the baby left the after-birth intact. Who would be more likely to commit such an act? A nervous paramedic candidate confronted with delivering a baby while its mother lay dying at her feet, or a seasoned Vietnam nurse and paramedic?

"Let me assure you, ladies and gentlemen of the jury: the kidnapper of this infant is sitting right before you. If Paramedic Beth Reilly had acted courageously, eighteen-year old Violet Williams might be nursing her infant. Instead, the young mother lies buried six-feet under, her baby stolen from her body with the deft cut of a surgical scissors.

Another crime will be committed, this time purely one of the heart, if you deny Mary Jean Williams a grandmother's claim on her own flesh and blood. As keepers of the law, your job is to prosecute Beth Reilly to the full limits of the law."

Flashing the jury a reassuring smile, the prosecuting attorney took his seat.

Jean pensively approached the jury, her arms clasped behind her. "Looks are deceiving, aren't they? But for slightly darkened hair and one-inch difference in height, my client and her paramedic officer looked remarkably similar, especially in a deep fog. Yet the state is asking you to trust the testimony of its sole eyewitness—a three-time petty thief scrounging a plea bargain—to prove beyond a reasonable doubt that my client was the paramedic responsible for kidnapping the baby she'd just delivered. I submit to the court that the paramedic Jerry Jablonski saw clutching a baby as she ran back to the ambulance was none other than Angie Ropella.

"At the time of the accident, Beth Reilly had only been a paramedic candidate with the Chicago Fire Department for six weeks, and in that time had never assisted in a birthing. Conversely, Angie Ropella had been a paramedic for fifteen years and a Vietnam nurse prior to that.

"My client already mentioned that Angie's coke habit flew under internal affairs radar because it never interfered with her job performance. A dark secret known, yet never divulged.

"In fact, up until the morning of that fateful accident, Angie Ropella's reputation as a paramedic had been exemplary, with several medals of valor to show for it. The horror she must have experienced after barreling her ambulance into a young woman, then causing her to go into labor and hemorrhage to death!

"Let's take a moment to review the details of the birthing: Angie kneels beside Beth to examine the victim; the mother is writhing in pain as the baby's head begins to crown, so the training officer prepares to deliver the baby.

"Concerned that Angie's hysteria will botch the delivery, Beth offers to assist, but Angie shoves her aside, ordering her to return to the ambulance for supplies. 'I'm not burying my career over a little mistake,' she screams.

"After wrapping the baby in a bloody sheet, Angie checks on the young mother, but she's beyond help. It starts to rain. Cradling the baby in one arm, she runs back to the ambulance, only to find her paramedic candidate attempting to radio-in for help. Climbing into the passenger's seat, Angie tears the radio from Beth's hands and tells her to drive. She places the baby between the front-seat armrests. They backtrack to the hospital for baby supplies. Later, Angie drops Beth off at McDonald's, cautioning her to keep her mouth shut. She returns twenty minutes later without the baby.

"Once back at the firehouse, Angie warns Beth to erase the accident from her mind, threatening to expose her in a modified diary entry of the morning's events.

Jean barreled into her conclusion. "Is Beth Reilly, a middle-aged paramedic candidate of six months, guilty of allowing her training officer to bully her into not reporting the accident? Yes. Is she guilty of leaving the scene of a hit-and-run? Yes. Is my client guilty of not pressing Angie for information regarding the baby's whereabouts? Yes again. But is Beth Reilly guilty of kidnapping and concealing a homicide? The answer is an unqualified no."

Slipping into her seat, Jean smiled reassuringly at Beth. "We just might have pulled it off," she whispered. But deep inside, she wasn't so sure.

Judge Dolan banged his gavel. "This court will take a twenty minute recess."

Reporters rushed out the doors, exposing a crowd of people milling around in the hall. Jean stood to stretch her legs, but Beth pulled her back down.

"Your attorney friend makes me sound like some kind of moral degenerate," she said anxiously.

"Your morals aren't on trial, you are. The state's job is to prove that, beyond a reasonable doubt, you were the person who kidnapped that baby. But all they have is the word of a three-time convicted petty thief who confused your ID photo with Angie's. Although your concoction of the McDonald's excursion was a bit far-fetched, I'd say you stand a good chance of being acquitted."

Beth was about to open her mouth in protest that the "excursion" was real, when her conscience kicked in. Hadn't Jean been on her side for the duration?

"I guess I did take it a bit too far," she said meekly.

"You have a fertile imagination," Jean observed wryly.

"What about Angie's diary?"

"That little gem about your captain confiscating the diary and attempting to blackmail you is hearsay, not allowed in court. As you recall, the judge ruled that Mr. Lamperi's statement be expunged from the record."

"But the jurors won't forget."

"That's a chance we have to take."

Chapter Twenty Seven

Judge Dolan glanced at the dozens of spectators and reporters filing into his courtroom. Quickly, he popped two antacids into his mouth and prepared to issue final instructions to the jury. Suddenly, a blue uniformed deputy sheriff suddenly burst through the double doors and headed toward the prosecuting attorney. After thrusting a sealed envelope into Jim's hand, the officer left.

A loud murmur arose in the courtroom.

"What is the meaning of this, Mr. Lamperi?" the judge thundered.

"If I may have a moment, your honor," said Jim, a disarming smile on his lips as he tore open the envelope and read the enclosed letter.

The noise level rose to a crescendo. "Silence!" warned the judge. "Make it fast Mr. Lamperi or I'll hold you in contempt of court."

Jean leaned toward Beth, who looked slightly flushed. "Probably one of his last minute tricks," she said.

"Well, Mr. Lamperi?" asked the judge.

Stifling a grin, Jim held the letter up for the jurors to see. "Your honor, we have a rebuttal witness."

"Have you forgotten, sir, that we are in final arguments?" the judge bellowed.

"Defense requests a mistrial!" Jean shouted.

"Both of you get up here now!"

The attorneys approached the bench.

"We need to talk to this Sue Dotson," said Jim.

"Your honor, this woman's name never appeared on the states' witness list,"

Jean protested.

"I had previously questioned this woman but was unaware until this very moment that she had decided to testify," said Jim.

"Exactly what part does this witness play, Mr. Lamperi?" asked the judge.

Jim paused for effect. "Sue Dotson knowingly acted as foster mother for the baby in question."

"Conjecture," Jean whispered angrily.

"Then we'll find that out when you cross-examine, won't we?" Jim asked innocently.

"Defense once again requests a mistrial."

Judge Dolan banged his gavel. "Slow down, both of you. A rebuttal witness is no reason for a mistrial. Fortunately for Mr. Lamperi, I haven't yet sequestered the jurors. We're going to finish this once and for all. Ms. Edgar, will Monday morning give you enough time to prepare?"

"Yes, your honor."

"Fine. And Mr. Lamperi, if you ever pull a stunt like this in my courtroom again, I'll have you disbarred."

"Yes, your honor," Jim said. Making his way past Jean, he whispered, "Gotcha!"

"This court is adjourned until 9:00 a.m. Monday."

Jean lifted her head from her desk, confronted by darkness. Wiping the sleep from her eyes, she gazed out her penthouse window onto Michigan Avenue. Except for a few Yellow Cabs streaming by, the streets were deserted. Fumbling for the chain on her tiffany lamp, she checked the wall clock. Great. She had to be in court in less than nine hours.

The attorney chastised herself for trusting the Beth to finally play by the rules. The paramedic was narcissistic enough to believe herself above the law. She had meekly weathered Jean's anger following the charade in the courtroom, then refused to see her attorney the rest of the week. A less-experienced lawyer might have withdrawn from the case, but Jean welcomed the challenge. She had no intention of abandoning her self-destructive client. So much for integrity.

Luckily, the coffee machine was still on. Emptying the remains of the pot into her mug, Jean thought about the promise she'd made to her new pastor when he'd hired her to represent Beth. "Spare no expense in defending the paramedic," Reverend Luke had said, "but give me your word that Sue Dotson will not be brought into this case."

"How is Sue Dotson connected to the paramedic?" Jean had asked.

"They've been best friends for the last twenty-five years," he'd answered in a tone that discouraged further discussion.

Accustomed to strange requests made by her Mafia-connected clientele, Jean had consented to the Reverend's request without giving it a second thought. Now her promise was coming back to haunt her. Still, the information she dug up on Sue Dotson in the last four days made her hands itch to get this woman on the stand. What kind of woman would jeopardize the lives of seven foster children by agreeing to raise a kidnapped infant, then sign-on with the prosecution when her best friend was brought to trial? So much for loyalty.

Yesterday, Jean had attended Sunday morning services at her new church. Reverend Luke introduced her to Sue, obviously unaware of her decision to testify for the state.

"So nice to meet you," Sue had said in a soft Southern drawl. Then she politely excused herself on pretext of retrieving her younger children from the nursery. Watching the Reverend's eyes follow Sue as she left the room, Jean sensed a sexual undertone to their relationship, at least on his end. No wonder he'd been so adamant about keeping her from testifying.

Later that day, when she told Revered Luke that Sue had contacted the prosecuting attorney, begging to testify, he flew into a rage, using expletives unbecoming to a man of the cloth. So much for morality.

Sipping the remains of the bitter coffee, Jean shivered in trepidation. A devout parishioner would disavow the counsel of her pastor only if the path he advised spelled out her spiritual demise! Sue would testify to avert eternal damnation. The fate of Beth, Baby Ruthie and Sue's foster children would come tumbling down, like a stack of dominoes unable to be rebuilt. So much for retribution.

* * *

The clerk held the King James Bible in front of the witness. "Do you swear to tell the whole truth, and nothing but the truth, so help you God?"

"To swear on the name of God is blasphemy," the petite, blond-haired woman replied.

The clerk removed the bible. "Do you solemnly affirm to tell the truth, the whole truth, and nothing but the truth?"

"I do."

Jim Lamperi approached the witness stand. "Please state your name for the court."

"Susan Ann Dotson.

"What is your occupation?"

"I'm a foster care mother."

"Licensed by the state of Illinois?"

"Yes."

"How long have you been in this occupation?"

"Eighteen years."

"How did you come into this line of work?"

"I married my husband right out of high school but we were unable to fulfill God's command to be fruitful and multiply."

"So you've filled your life with other peoples' children."

"They are my solace."

"Approximately how many foster children have passed through your doors over the years?"

"Seventy-nine children," Sue said proudly.

"And the children arrive with identification and medical history?"

"Goodness, it sounds like you all are talking about buying a car."

"Sorry. Is it safe to assume that you receive all relevant data concerning the children before you accept them into your home?"

"That is correct."

"Do all of these children come to you through DCFS?"

Sue shook her head. "I receive my children through the church but DCFS oversees their care."

"Have you ever had occasion to receive a child from an independent source?"

"Yes."

"Through a friend?"

"Your honor, counsel is leading the witness," Jean said.

"Sustained. Let the question be stricken from the record."

"Ms. Dotson, can you describe an occasion when you have received a child through an independent source?" Jim asked patiently.

Sue drew a pale pink tissue from her purse. "A friend recently placed a baby in my charge."

"Was it her baby?"

Sue cast her eyes down. "No, sir."

"Whose baby was it?"

"That of an unfortunate girl who was killed in a hit-and-run."

"Was your friend in some way related to this girl?"

"No sir."

"Then how is it that she came to be in possession of this baby?"

"She was riding with her paramedic officer when their ambulance hit a pregnant homeless girl. The girl went into labor. My friend said she was able to deliver the infant, but she couldn't save the mother. She said that DCFS would have a difficult time placing a bi-racial infant, so she brought the infant to my door."

"So your friend kidnapped the baby in question?"

"Objection! Counsel is asking the witness to make a legal conclusion," Jean interjected.

"Sustained. Mr. Lamperi, you will kindly keep these inflammatory words to yourself."

"I must bear witness, your honor. My friend did kidnap that baby and deliver her to me. But she thought she was helping the child."

"Praise the Lord!" a voice rang through the courtroom.

"Sexual and physical abuse of foster children runs rampant throughout the system," continued Sue.

"Silence in the court," roared the judge.

"Is your friend in this courtroom today?" Jim continued.

"Yes sir, she is."

"Can you point your friend out to us, Ms. Dotson?"

Breaking into tears, Sue pointed in Beth's direction. "God forgive you!"

"No further questions, your honor."

The silence was so deafening that the sound of chair legs grating across the floor could be heard across the courtroom. Pushing her chair back, Jean arose from behind the table to cross-examine the witness.

"How long have you known Beth Reilly?" asked the state's attorney.

"Since high school." Sue blew her nose.

"So that's about fifteen years ago?"

A watery smile broke through the tears. "You're being kind. Beth and I have been friends for twenty-five years."

"Can you describe your relationship with my client?"

"She was a darling. And sharp as a tack. She pushed me to develop my interest in art and design."

"How did you two meet?"

"My family moved here from North Carolina when I was in high school. I was shy and kept to myself. One day in biology class, I was having an awful time cutting up a snake when out of the blue, this girl sat down and helped me. From then on, we were best friends She introduced me to the other kids, and tutored me in math and science. She even talked my mother into allowing me try out for cheerleading."

"An interest you both shared?"

"Not one bit. Beth was involved with the Animal Rights and Save Our Planet organizations. But she knew I really wanted to try out for cheerleading so she cast her magic wand."

"A loyal friend."

"Oh, yes."

"A good friend is truly a gem," quoted Jean.

"Praise the Lord."

"In all the years you've known her, has Beth ever asked you to participate in an illegal act?"

"She allowed me to take part in her adventures, like signing a phony absence slip to hand in to her teachers while she was out rescuing dogs about to be euthanized."

"How did her parents react to her behavior?"

"They never suspected. They were both professors at the university. As long as she brought home 'straight A's', they never questioned her about her comings and goings."

"Earlier, you said you forged Beth's parents' names on excuse slips for school."

"Objection, your honor," the prosecuting attorney protested. "The word *forged* connotes illegal activity."

"I'll rephrase, your honor. You said you signed 'excuse slips' for Beth."

"That's right."

"At any time, did Beth force you to cover for her?"

"She didn't have to. I loved being part of the excitement she generated."

"Did it bother you that signing her parents' names on those excuse slips might be illegal?"

"Not then, but it would bother me now."

"Why is that?"

"I've met the Lord. Anything like that would be considered dishonest."

"Amen, sister," came a voice from the rear of the room.

"Guard, please escort the woman in the back row from the room," the judge ordered.

"Yet you had no moral dilemma concealing a kidnapped infant," Jean said, her tone suddenly razor-sharp.

"That's not true! I knew it was morally wrong but Beth was my best friend, she needed me."

"So whenever someone asks you for help, you acquiesce?"

"Of course not, but she said the Lord had delivered that infant unto me, that she would only languish at DCFS."

"So you were just being a good Samaritan by taking in this baby."

"I was just doing God's work. The baby's mother was a homeless child, herself."

Jean thrust a pocket-sized book into Sue's hands. "On what page does the Bible condone stealing another woman's child?"

Sue covered her eyes with her hands.

"Isn't it true, Ms. Dotson, that you accepted that baby in exchange for the one you aborted years ago?"

"How did you—?" Sue screamed, her eyes widening in disbelief at Reverend Luke smugly smiling at her from across the courtroom.

"During the last six months, you could have anonymously contacted the police on numerous occasions. Instead you flagrantly put the lives of your seven foster children at risk by aiding and abetting a kidnapping."

"Objection, your honor. Counsel is badgering the witness."

"Overruled."

"After a while, you began to think of that baby as your own. When Beth appealed to you for emotional support, you abandoned her as you would a leper"

Beth jumped to her feet and shouted, "It's all right, Sue. I understand!"

The judge banged his gavel. "The defendant will be seated!"

"Little did my client know she had a Judas in her midst," Jean said disgustedly.

"Objection!" Jim Lamperi was on his feet.

"I may be a charlatan," sobbed Sue, "but I refuse to be eternally damned for not coming forth and speaking God's truth!"

Judge Dolan was furiously banging his gavel but Jean was too incensed to cease her verbal attack on this silly woman.

"Never once during this trial did Beth mention your name, even though she had no one to testify on her behalf. She kept silent so that you, your foster children, and the newest addition to your family would be safe. That's friendship. No further questions, your honor."

Jean briskly returned to her seat, the sight of her client's silent tears tearing at her heart.

Chapter Twenty Eight

Monroe wiped the sweat from his forehead as Maggie served the next ball. Running to meet it, he slammed it right back. Maggie's racquet caught the ball on a curve and yanked it down.

"One for the paramedic," laughed Monroe, serving the ball once again.

"You got that right," shouted Maggie, slamming the ball against the wall. "Who would have thought she'd finally be put away?"

"All because that holy-roller bulldozed her way into the courtroom."

"That little escapade must have driven the defense nuts."

"Reilly had no choice but to plead guilty and beg for mercy."

"It was like a goddam soap-opera, what with that Reverend Luke boasting that he gave Sue Dotson 'permission' to conceal that baby," said Maggie, bending for the ball.

"A real man of the cloth." Monroe said.

"The devil's cloth."

"And all Dotson gets is counseling and community service. What's that all about?"

Maggie tossed a towel over her shoulders and headed for the door. "Reilly sure as hell didn't show any remorse over kidnapping that baby."

"If anything, she seemed more upset that her best friend and all those foster kids had to be dragged into it."

"What ever happened to the foster kids?" asked Monroe, meeting his partner's stride.

"This Reverend Luke guy was adamant about trying to find homes for them among his parishioners, but the court turned the kids over to DCFS. Who can trust a guy who's got the morals of a sewer rat? Anyway, he's got his own problems."

"Isn't he the pastor whose church funded that abortion clinic bombing in Florida?"

"That's what they say," said Maggie, slamming the tennis ball over the net. "You ask me, he's the one who should have been charged as an accomplice

in the kidnapping.

"Well, at least baby and grandma are reunited."

"That's one gutsy woman, speaking out against the injustices her husband committed against both her and her daughter, then accepting a biracial grandchild."

"All this time, John Paul Williams was denying the morgue photograph was his daughter because he thought the baby was his," Monroe said, smirking.

"Must have been a bombshell when his sons told him Violet got it on with a black guy who worked the merry-go-round for a traveling carnival."

"And Violet's brothers are siding with their father."

"Let's just say they don't want their mom back anytime soon."

"Hey, maybe Sue Dotson can baby-sit for grandma while she tries to find a job in Chicago!" suggested Monroe.

"You're sick, you know that?"

They both laughed.

"I'm sorry it worked out this way," said Jean, pressing Beth to her.

Although Jean felt tears on her blouse, Beth was rigid in her arms.

Taking a deep breath, Jean said, "I've known the truth about Sue and Baby Ruth all along."

Beth looked up. "How?"

"Reverend Luke apprised me of all the facts when he hired me to defend you. His only stipulation was that I not drag Sue into the case. As an attorney, I couldn't breach his confidence. I had hoped that you would confide in me about the kidnapping. Then we would have had ammunition to use on the stand. But when it came to your best friend, you chose the strong, silent approach. Too bad your friend didn't feel the same way when it came to you."

Beth cried softly. "We were almost all home free. I still can't believe she testified."

"Since you've been incarcerated, your friend has been living a dream of denial. She broke off her relationship with you, fantasizing that the infant was actually hers."

"Out of sight, out of mind," whispered Beth.

"Exactly. And she was almost home free until the DCFS worker made a surprise visit and started questioning the baby's identity. At that point, the floodwaters broke and the Sue you knew was washed away."

"What do you mean?"

"Sue felt her spirit under siege. She must clear her conscience or remain the devil's disciple for evermore. Friendship, loyalty, and the children's well-being were no longer of utmost importance."

"Meanwhile leaving the rest of us to be swept away in the current. You know, whether or not your analysis is entirely correct, you helped me see Sue's motives."

"I still don't completely understand your motives for kidnapping that baby and leaving her mother to die."

"What's to understand? I was a walking time-bomb: middle-aged, infertile, no guy in the picture, abruptly orphaned. Through a twist of fate, a baby literally pops into my waiting arms. I seize the day! I'm a hero, protecting a bi-racial baby from languishing at DCFS! Giving that baby a loving home."

Jean looked at Beth in astonishment. "But you could have let me plead temporary insanity."

"Was it insane to single-handedly change the life of an abandoned baby?"

"I'd venture that kidnapping a baby not of your own body to create an instant family could certainly be termed temporary insanity. Also, that abandonment label is a bit harsh; you never even bothered to check the familial background of that child."

Beth sighed. "Please stop pushing, Jean. I'm done playing the What if? game."

"Speaking of playing, your friend certainly played the jurors' emotions like a pro. Maybe she should run for office after she finishes her five-hundred hours of community service."

Beth smiled grimly. "She'll probably run to Bosnia. She always wanted to be a missionary. Too bad the kids got caught in the line of fire."

"Any regrets?"

Beth shook her head. "Sue always wanted a baby."

"You never intended to give the baby to Sue, did you Beth?" Jean asked gently.

Beth shook her head. "I thought she'd put the baby up for adoption through Reverend Luke."

"I'd say you took that baby to raise as your own."

Beth smiled sadly. "What difference does it make now?"

"Despite all your efforts, you've lost the baby and your best friend."

"At least Baby Ruthie connected with her grandma," Beth said.

"You'll probably be out on parole in less than five years. I suggest you use your time of confinement wisely."

"Wisely'?"

Jean covered Beth's hand with her own. "You're all sharp edges on the outside, but a lonely little child on the inside. Try to cut through that barbed wire and rescue the loving person underneath all that debris."

"More psycho-babble," Beth smiled.

"Listen, it's never too late to change. Goodbye Beth, and good luck." Jean gave her a squeeze and called for the guard. The steel door slammed behind her.

Once the cell door locked, Beth's smile quickly faded. Abandoned yet again. She hung her head to cry.

A key rattled her cell lock. Startled, Beth raised her head. "You up for a visitor, Reilly? Dude with a beard."

Beth nodded, swiping at her tears. Maybe not forsaken after all.

Chapter Twenty Nine

Drunken applause accompanied Jim Lamperi as he stumbled off the Karaoke stage and into the arms of the petite brunette whom he'd met earlier that evening.

"You were wonderful!" she gushed, taking his hand and leading him through a smoky maze of bodies. When they approached a table at the rear of the bar, she nudged him with her hip and he fell into his chair.

A young Oriental man at the next table, his black hair fastened into a shoulder length ponytail, stood up to shake Jim's hand. "Those gyrations you did when you sang 'I Did It My Way' were really cool. Just like that guy from the Fifties, right?"

"Right," Jim mumbled, turning back to his table. Fumbling in his pockets, he pulled out a cigarette.

"Here, let me," said the brunette, flicking a gold cigarette lighter emblazoned with an *M*. "Another beer?"

"Sure, why not?" Jim said.

She beckoned to a bar maid in black silk shorts. "So tell me, how did you get to become a judge?" she asked, pushing a folded bill into the bar maid's hand.

Jim offered her a cigarette. "I was working my butt off when this paramedic hit-and-run case came along."

"I remember seeing that story a few weeks ago on the news. A real soap opera."

Jim flicked the dead ashes on the lacquered wooden table.

"Listen, why don't you and I disappear to someplace more intimate?"

"Maybe later." She batted her eyelashes at him. "I'm just dying to hear what finally happened to the baby."

Jim slurped from his frothy beer mug. "Winds up the best friend is a born-again Christian in the throes of a spiritual dilemma. She confides in her pastor. He tells her not to worry, that she acted in the Lord's name.

"The paramedic is brought to trial. He denies knowing anything about a missing baby. All bases are loaded in the kidnapper's favor, and it's the bottom of the ninth inning."

"What did you do?"

"Used my ace in the hole guaranteed to land me a juvenile court judgeship."

"The paramedic's best friend?"

Jim shook his head. "The Reverend. He'd been trying to get into his favorite parishioner's knickers for years. Thought he'd score some points by keeping her name out of the case. Never guessed she'd crawl out of the woodwork and testify against her best friend. Once the distinguished Reverend figured out the score, he contacted me himself, sharing some choice tidbits concerning an abortion performed long ago."

"On Sue Dotson?"

"One and the same."

"I thought men of the cloth could be trusted to keep secrets."

"Revenge trumps all. Anyway, both he and Sue's best friend got more than they bargained for."

"What happened to the paramedic?" the brunette asked, toying with the lighter.

"She got five years in prison."

"And the reverend?"

"Seems the guy was involved in funding a recent abortion clinic bombing in Florida."

"The one killing a doctor and nurse?"

"One and the same. When it came to kabooming abortion clinics, he was no virgin. Even the church elders knew of his activities. The only one left in the dark was—"

"Sue Dotson."

"You got it. All these months, she'd been wrestling with her conscience about her part in the kidnapping scheme. Then a DCFS worker questions the baby's identity and she's about to teeter. Who does she call?"

"Her pastor?"

"Right again. She tells him she never procured a fake birth certificate for the baby. He flies into a rage. The adoption will be traced to him, the church's undercover funding of abortion clinic bombings revealed."

"How does Sue react?"

"Next morning she's in my office blabbering about the kidnapping, as well as Reverend Luke's illegal escapades."

"How come the church didn't fire the guy?"

"He was a charismatic speaker, church membership at an all-time high."

"So what's going to happen to him?"

Jim eyed the gold lighter reflected on the laminated tabletop. "You sure ask a lot of questions, even for a broad."

"I'm just interested in current events," she smiled demurely.

Suddenly his antenna went up. "Hey, what did you say you do for a living?"

Securely tucking the lighter into her black handbag, the brunette stood up casually. "I've got to use the little girl's room."

"Hey, wait a minute." He got up, staggering after her. By the time he'd pushed through the large group of people waiting in line, the woman had disappeared. He yanked open the l adies room door. There were squeals of protest, but no sight of the petite brunette with whom he'd spent the evening.

The woman slipped out the front door and into the night. Pulling a cellular phone from her purse, she punched in some numbers. "Harry? Have I got a juicy story for you."

~End~

About the Author

Jennie Spallone is past president of Off-campus Writer's Workshop, a 250-member writers group located in Winnetka, IL. A freelance journalist of thirteen years, Spallone has written over one-hundred profiles and feature stories for local and national publications. She recently spoke on the New Authors' Panel at the LOVE IS MURDER mystery writing conference in Rosemont, IL. Spallone, a member of Sisters in Crime, recently received a certificate of recognition for her participation in a twelve-Week Citizens Fire Academy.

Her non-fiction books include WRITE ME UP! a written expression program for students with special needs, and GRASPING GRAMMAR! a multisensory approach to teaching grammar. She can be reached at

~~http://www.Jennie~~ spalloneauthor@aol.com.